WORTH THE COMING HOME

LISA M. OWENS

Dreamspinner Press

Published by
Dreamspinner Press
5032 Capital Circle SW
Ste 2, PMB# 279
Tallahassee, FL 32305-7886
USA
http://www.dreamspinnerpress.com/

Worth the Coming Home

Cover Art by Anne Cain
annecain.art@gmail.com

ISBN: 978-1-62380-044-4

Printed in the United States of America
First Edition
October 2012

eBook edition available
eBook ISBN: 978-1-62380-045-1

For Edwin and Eric, who helped me start,
And for Eva, who made sure I finished.

Acknowledgments

WRITING is a solitary craft, yet I have been blessed in both my nonfiction and fiction careers to find great companies of fellow writers who have taught and encouraged me. My fiction critique group in Columbus, Ohio—Abbie, Eva, Sarah, and Randi—supported the creation of *Worth the Coming Home* from beginning to end and read every word multiple times. I hope you each know how very dear you are to me and how much I miss seeing you. Thanks to Holly, who let me join her on her long-ago romance review blog—it's where I learned so much by reading so much more; to Heidi, Doris, Rusti, and Glenn, and my Aunts Boots and Donna, who were my first fans; to Pam and Margo for being my first readers, and Marsha for being my last; to Lynn at Sparkling Dawg for my fabulous website; to Connie, my own personal Horse Whisperer; and to Debbie Phillips and Andrea Dowding of Women on Fire (www.beawomanonfire.com). I was fortunate to be in a WOF group, trying to figure out my next dream, when a layoff ended my newspaper career. WOF helped me realize I could write a novel and I could move to Montana. My wonderful husband agreed, and here we are.

Thanks to my great virtual support group—the members of the Rainbow Romance Writers, the LGBT chapter of Romance Writers of America. If you love male/male and LGBT romance, you can't do better than to visit our website, www.rainbowromancewriters.com, review the members list, and then check out any of our websites and books. These are the writers I love to read, and I have learned so very much from them about writing, the business of writing, and how to be professional doing it. If you're a reader who wants to become a romance writer, the best thing you can do is join Romance Writers of America and then join your local or our specialty chapter.

Thank you, too, to everyone at Dreamspinner Press: Elizabeth North, artist Anne Cain—who made Josh and Dane look like they always looked to me—and the great editing team. I am so grateful I landed in your capable hands.

.

ONE

"DAMN it, Josh. Are you training that horse or dancing with him? You know Hanson will be running his mouth all over the valley about your lack of skill if it bests you."

My brother's taunts flew like the dust the mustang was kicking up. Problem was, Jesse sat high on the fence while I stood down in the mess in the corral.

The gelding ran from me the minute I stepped into the enclosure, and it didn't help that I missed the first time I tried to throw a rope around his neck. Now he was at the far end with his butt facing me. Not the end a trainer wants to see.

"I told you, you were a moron to buy this animal," Jesse continued. "There's no way Hanson will take him back."

I didn't care about the money. I didn't want to fail this horse. He was beautiful. About two years old, all black, with a thick mane and tail. Perfect head and chest, strong legs, on the tall side, which suited me. Proud, courageous, and totally wild. I had to figure a way to start him.

Damn that jackass Ray Hanson. Normally, I don't swear—my mom didn't like it. But what else are you going to call a man who tries to train a smart horse the dumb way?

Ray had invited me over to watch him start the mustang. He's always wanted folks to think he's better than me with horses. He's got some strengths of his own. Me? I just understand horses. I can't explain it. Maybe I got it from my dad. Folks have told me he was the best.

I'd wanted to work with a wild mustang all my life, so I went to Hanson's place when he called. Right off, it was bad. The horse was real smart. But bad things had been done to him in the short time he'd been around humans.

Hanson did more when he put the halter on. Walked right up to the animal, put a chokehold on his neck, and had his foreman force the halter on. It was violent and ugly, and the horse's eyes turned dark and hard. Hanson was in real danger of taking everything gorgeous out of that animal and breaking his spirit for good.

Soon the man was in danger period. The gelding's ears went flat against his neck, and he struck at Hanson with both front legs. Then he ran. When he couldn't escape, he let his back hooves fly to keep Hanson away. Hanson got mad and called for his rifle, and that's when I bought him.

Before the next morning, Hanson had told everybody at Cunningham's Bar and Grill how he'd planned all along to sell me an unbreakable horse at a profit. Now I had to make progress or I'd be hearing about how Hanson had bested me from every cowboy in the valley, especially my brother. Sometimes Jesse played his older brother card too hard. Yeah, he had five years on me. But I was twenty-five now, and I didn't see five years as any big age difference anymore. I'd graduated college, and I was a respected horse breeder and trainer. It was time Jesse noticed.

I picked up the tail of my halter rope and tossed the rope toward the mustang's hindquarters. It fell harmlessly to the ground, which is what I wanted. But the horse ignored it, which I didn't want.

I pulled the halter rope in and threw it again and again for nearly half an hour. I needed to turn his front quarters toward me. Finally, as I pulled it toward me once more, the gelding turned his head to look at me. He studied me a long time, making a decision.

Sweat rolled down my neck and pooled on my lower back. I took a slow, controlled breath and waited. His ears twitched and his nostrils flared, like he was catching my scent. He took a step toward me and licked his lips.

It was the reaction I was looking for. Carefully, I closed the distance between us, keeping myself in his line of sight. The mustang flicked his ears and bowed his neck, wanting to leave but unsure he needed to. I stopped, letting him make the decision to stay. He didn't, but I started my approach again. He still distrusted me, and I paused again, and then we continued the dance until I was beside him.

I lifted my hand in the air as if to stroke his neck, but I didn't touch him, and we repeated that until, at last, he accepted my caress. Murmuring softly, I apologized to him for all the errors others had made.

"That's it. Feels good, doesn't it?" I whispered low, making him strain to hear me as I stroked him. "You're in a better place now. You realize that, don't you, Hurricane? That's what I'm naming you, okay? Because you kick up such a fuss. We're going to have a good time together."

Next, I rubbed his withers and shoulders, firm enough so he knew he didn't need to be afraid of my touch. Hurricane took the halter, then began to respond to the pressure of the rope. If my luck held out, he'd be taking a saddle in no time.

"Well, I'll be damned," Jesse said. "I didn't believe you could do even that with that animal. Good work, Josh."

"Quite a show," a voice called from the driveway.

A stranger was coming toward us, moving like he hadn't walked in days. Judging by the dust on the black Silverado behind him, maybe he hadn't. His hair was a little on the long side for southwestern Montana, and he was maybe four inches taller than me. He wore jeans and combat boots, and he had muscles everywhere, bulging along his arms and legs and all controlled tight and held ready under his camo T-shirt.

He nodded at me, then stared at Jesse. My brother had turned around to look at him, but now he jumped off the fence and ran at him. He stopped short in front of him, looking him over, then hugged him hard.

"Took you long enough to get here."

The stranger let go in Jesse's arms, like a balloon you let all the air out of. Then he sucked it all back in quick. Pulling himself together, he stepped back and looked my brother over, not saying a word. The two of them were nearly the same size, except the stranger had more muscle. And he had dark hair, while my brother's was short and blond like mine.

"Damn, Dane, it's good to see you," Jesse said. His grin was huge when he turned to me. "Josh, this is my old Ranger buddy, Dane Keller."

"Good to meet you," I called out in a low voice, still rubbing and monitoring Hurricane. "Let me finish with my horse."

"We made good progress, Hurricane." I gave him one last rub and turned away, keeping him in my peripheral vision as I made my way to the gate. Hurricane's ears and eyes focused on my leaving, and it was satisfying to watch.

Now I could turn my attention to the stranger. He gripped my hand when we shook, in the way of men used to commanding attention and others.

"Good to meet you, little brother. That was some work with the horse."

Even when giving the compliment, Dane's voice was deep and controlled, like he was used to controlling everything all the time. His gray eyes never wavered as he studied my face, and that and his grip and his voice made my stomach flip. God, I wanted him to touch me all over.

"How long were you watching?"

"Long enough to know you knew what you were doing."

"Thanks. I—"

"Dane," Jesse interrupted. "Come on up to the house. You look like you could use a beer. How long can you stay?"

Slapping Dane's shoulder, Jesse turned him toward his house. "Come on along, Josh," he added.

"Give me a few minutes," I said to his back. "Aunt Kate wanted to talk to me before the guest cookout." Brooks Ranch was a working cattle and horse ranch that took guests in summer. It had been that way for a hundred years.

"Good. You can make us some dinner then," he replied.

ABOUT twenty minutes later, I found them drinking on Jesse's deck. The sun was slipping behind the Gallatin Range on the west side of the valley, throwing pink highlights across the Absaroka Mountains behind the ranch. The light made the alfalfa and pines and cottonwoods glow so the whole valley really looked like its name implied: Paradise. It was my favorite time of day, and I couldn't imagine a better place in the world to be, ever.

Dane and Jesse had served together in Afghanistan and Iraq. Jesse said Dane saved his life a couple of times, and when Dane stayed in the Army, they stayed in touch.

"I didn't re-up, Jesse," Dane said as I stepped onto the deck. Dane took a long drink from his beer, and Jesse studied him hard.

"Good," my brother said. "What you going to do?"

Dane stared at his beer can for a bit, then shrugged. "I don't know. Got all my gear in the truck. Left Bragg a couple days ago, and here I am." He tried to grin, but it wasn't working. It was like his muscles had forgotten how.

"Good," Jesse said again. "You rest up a couple days. Uncle Karl can put you to work, and you can stay with me. We can get some fishing in."

"Still got a plan for everything, hey?" Dane said, shaking his head.

I had to laugh at that, and they both noticed I was there. Dane looked at me, and this time he almost smiled. It sent a thrill through me.

"You do know my brother."

"That's right," Jesse said. "You two make fun. But I do have a plan, and the next part involves you making a decent welcome home dinner, Josh, while we bring in Dane's gear."

"Yes, sir. Right away, sir." I saluted. Jesse whipped me the finger, and they headed toward the Silverado.

I am a pretty good cook. Started helping my mom when I was little, then helped cook for guests after our parents died and Uncle Karl and Aunt Kate took us in.

Tonight I wanted to make something really good to impress Dane. But I couldn't take a lot of time. I settled for homemade meatballs and a doctored-up jar of spaghetti sauce, plus salad and my own version of garlic bread using store-bought bread. It all smelled pretty good when I took it out to the deck.

As usual, Jesse ate fast. Dane seemed to be enjoying every bite. I liked that.

"I haven't had a meal like this in forever, Josh," he said, looking me in the face as he wiped at his mouth with a napkin. "Thank you."

Later that night, lying in bed at my cabin, I thought about that compliment and the look in Dane's eyes. Was he gay? If I let myself, I could want him bad, just like I wanted to train the horse.

I sighed and folded my hands behind my head. No use getting my hopes up. Even if he was interested, how could I do anything about it when no one knew the truth about me?

TWO

THE next morning, I stopped by Jesse's early. I was surprised to find Dane already up and the coffee made.

"Good stuff. Thanks."

"Jesse doesn't make coffee, does he?"

"Heck no. Loves to drink it but won't make it. Says he's biologically unable. You want me to make breakfast?" I rummaged through the refrigerator. "Eggs and bacon okay? You want scrambled or something else?"

"Eggs any way is great," he replied, leaning against the counter and stretching out his long legs. I forced myself to look away. "Your brother really, really cannot make coffee. It tastes like shit."

"And here I thought he was lying to get out of helping." I started cracking eggs in a bowl, but I wanted to keep the conversation going. "So you're done with the Rangers for good?"

"Yes."

"You must have seen some interesting stuff."

"Interesting," he repeated. "Let's change the subject." His face was expressionless.

"Sure. Sorry...." I felt stupid, but I didn't want him to stop talking. "You given any thought to what you want to do today? Jesse is heading into Billings to check out an auction, but it's four hours there and back."

"I don't think I want to spend much more time in a truck ride right away." Dane took a long drink of his coffee and aimed his penetrating stare at me. "What are you doing today?"

He was interested? Too bad I wasn't doing anything exciting. "I'm leading a trail ride for kids right after lunch."

"What are you doing until lunch?"

"Getting horses ready for the trail ride."

He was quiet for a few minutes. I put the bacon in the skillet and concentrated on not splashing grease on myself.

"Where's the plates and silverware?"

I pointed and he started setting the table.

"Mind if I tag along on your ride?"

I felt compelled to turn around. He was staring at me again. Suddenly, my pants were too tight and my face heated. I turned back to the stove.

"Not at all. You ridden much?"

"I've ridden."

"How about herding kids?"

"Some." He paused awhile, like he was remembering something. "I can lift them on and off the horses at least."

"You're on. We'll head over to the barn after breakfast and get you familiar with the saddle again. Then we'll get the horses ready for the kids, have lunch, and hit the trail."

A thundering on the stairs announced Jesse was up. Dane poured a new cup of coffee and held it out as my brother walked through the doorway.

"Thanks. How'd you sleep, Dane?"

"It's quiet here."

"Yeah. Not much going on unless the wind is blowing, and that's the way we like it. You making bacon and eggs, Josh?"

"Scrambled."

"Good. Make sure everybody takes raincoats on this afternoon's ride. It's a real possibility you'll need them." He turned to Dane. "What you thinking about doing today? And nothing is an option."

"Going along on Josh's trail ride."

"Great idea," Jesse answered, not missing a beat. "Try not to swear around the kids. Uncle Karl doesn't like it. It was hard for me to stop after I got home."

"Got it."

I put breakfast on the table and headed for the barn. I'd just finished saddling Hector when Dane joined me. He had a small pack slung over his shoulder.

"If it's okay with you, I'm going to put you on Sugarpie."

"Sugarpie?"

"She's a good, gentle horse for a trail ride with kids," I said, but I could feel heat rising up my neck and face. The guy made me too self-conscious about everything. "My mother named her."

"What's your horse called?"

"Hector."

"Hector."

"He was born when I was studying Greek mythology." Even to me, I sounded lame.

"And I'm on Sugarpie."

I looked away. I couldn't think of a thing to say. Probably one of the reasons I spent so much time with horses.

"Relax. Sugarpie is fine."

"Okay then."

I led the horses out of the barn and handed off Sugarpie's reins. Dane swung smoothly into the saddle and settled in. I mounted and we took off at a walk.

"We won't go much faster than this all afternoon. But feel free to ease into a lope when you're ready."

I stayed behind Dane awhile, as I do nearly every time I'm with a rider new to me. Usually, I watch for the person to get comfortable. And I watched for that with Dane. But I was watching his tight butt and the way it rocked with the horse, like sex with clothes on, just as much.

He was uneasy in the saddle at first, but I could see him trying hard to listen to what Sugarpie was telling him. Then came the moment everything clicked. One second he was stiff and Sugarpie was tense. The next, Dane moved with her, and Sugarpie perked up like she might have a good time after all. I watched the smooth rocking a few minutes longer, until my jeans were painfully tight. Then I had to wait until I'd calmed down some so I could move up to join him.

"You're doing really good. Caught on again really fast."

"Thanks, cowboy."

I didn't like the nickname, but I bit my tongue. As we rounded the big curve that separated my and Jesse's places from where my aunt and uncle lived, I stopped and became tour guide, pointing out the structures around us. The ranch was tucked into that space where the tilled, green fields of the valley meet the steady, forested slope that stretches up to the sharp rocky peaks of the Absarokas. The scene was like a picture postcard, and we used it in our advertising.

"That's the big house." I pointed to the long, rambling, two-story log home. "It's the original homestead from when my great-great-grandfather claimed the first couple hundred acres. Added onto, of course, once he decided to turn the place into a dude ranch. I'll show you the great hall and dining room at lunch. The woodwork is really something.

"We've turned some of the old family bedrooms into guest suites. My aunt and uncle live there, and it's a place for guests to eat, relax, and hang out. There's a nice library too.

"To the right are corrals and the big horse barn. We keep about twenty-five horses, give or take, for guests and family. Beyond the horse barn, in the pines, are five guest cabins and the swim pond. And opposite the horse barn are the corrals and barns for the cattle and a bunkhouse for the hands. We have two full-time and add some in summer. Plus locals who help with the work at the big house during guest season."

"It all looks pretty from up here. You still running black Angus?"

"How'd you know that?"

Dane took a minute to answer, like he was embarrassed. "Your letters to your brother when we were in Afghanistan," he said at last. "And your brother talked about it too."

"Jesse's in charge of the cattle now, about two hundred fifty head. We're a seed stock operation, breeding top of the line cows for ranchers who want to improve their herds."

Dane nodded.

"Well, enough of that, I guess. Let's head for the guest corral."

A Montana rancher doesn't normally blurt out much of anything about his operation, but I wanted Dane to know enough to appreciate the ranch and maybe stay awhile.

"What are you in charge of?"

"The horses. I buy, breed, and train them. Run the trail rides and teach guests to ride. I teach some local people too, and train horses for folks around the valley." It was my standard answer.

"Why'd you choose the horse you were training yesterday?"

"Because I didn't want Ray Hanson to have him."

"And Ray Hanson is?"

"A guy who thinks he's the best horse trainer on earth."

"Competition?"

"I don't see it that way, but he does. I wish he didn't."

Dane was quiet then, and kicked Sugarpie into a lope. Sugarpie and Hector were happy to speed up, and we reached the corral fast. Dang, Dane looked good on a horse.

"And you and Jesse each have your own place?" he asked as we dismounted.

"Yeah, he lives in the house our parents built, and I live in the cabin that was my grandmother's after Grandpa died. A couple years back, I decided I... wanted some privacy from all Jesse's girlfriends."

"He does have a way with the ladies. That run in the family, cowboy?"

"Not so much," I mumbled. Did he think I was straight?

We left our mounts in the corral and entered the barn, where I gathered up the gear for brushing the horses the kids would ride and gave him some pointers. He nodded and went to work. It was clear he'd done it before, and I left him alone pretty quickly.

I started my work at the other end of the building, working back toward him. When I returned, he was brushing Moonstruck, a pretty chestnut mare with a white crescent on her forehead. I stopped opposite him on her other side.

"You're doing great."

"I'll bet you say that to all the guys you talk into this job," Dane said. He didn't look at me, just kept brushing Moonstruck's side, his left arm resting on her back.

Tentatively, I reached out and grazed his forearm. I wanted to brush it like he was brushing Moonstruck, to feel the muscles under his tanned skin, but I kept my hand still.

I pretended I was studying the tattoo on his forearm. It was hard to miss: a grinning skull wearing sunglasses. "Rangers" was inscribed below it, and underneath that were two crossed daggers.

"No, really, I'm serious." I wished I could think up something better.

He stopped brushing and straightened up. I moved my hand to Moonstruck's back, trying to appear like it was casual.

"I know you are, cowboy."

"You going to keep calling me that?"

"I might."

"And if I told you I didn't like it?"

He laughed. "I'd call you cowboy all the time. You want to tell me something now, cowboy?" he challenged.

"No." My answer was too quick. When he raised an eyebrow at me, I knew he knew it too. He was quiet for a minute, but he never stopped grinning or looking at me. Then he changed the subject in a way that had me nearly squirming.

"So when did you realize you loved... horses?"

What the heck?

I tried real hard to act like I hadn't noticed his hesitation. I wanted too badly to read something into it. But I had to answer his question too, and soon. I went for a safe answer.

"When I was real little. Dad sat me on a horse when I was two. I had my own pony when I was four. Pokey. I taught her a few tricks, and it just went from there."

"Tricks?"

"Yeah, jumping small things, rearing on command, taking a couple steps with me standing on her back. Lone Ranger stuff."

"You were the Lone Ranger?"

"Not really. Mainly, you know, I was trying to impress my parents and brother. Mom thought I was awesome. Jesse teased me something fierce. It was all typical stuff." Boy, I sounded stupid.

"More like special, I'm thinking."

He's done this a hundred times. The thought popped aloud into my head like someone had spoken it. I was out of my league. I'd screwed around with a gang of gay friends in college, but suddenly I wasn't sure what to do next. I wasn't sure "next" was even a smart thing to do.

"I suppose," Dane said quietly, "we should finish this up and go get some lunch and our riders."

"Yeah." I slid my hand down Moonstruck's leg to check her feet, and blood pounded in my head. Both of them. My cock felt like it would never go soft again. I heard him gather up the brushes and move to the next stall.

WHEN we got to the big house, Aunt Kate and my best friend Sarah were serving lunch to the kids. A high school English teacher, Sarah ran our kids programs in summer.

I introduced Dane, and Aunt Kate put us to work fetching pans of food for the late lunch seating, mainly the fly-fishing and hiking crowd. When we'd finished that, she sent us off to Uncle Karl.

On the way, we stopped in the great hall so Dane could see the woodwork my great-great-grandfather had created. The room was forty by forty, with a bank of large windows on each of the two outside walls. Carved fluted columns and rosettes in contrasting woods framed each window, and the pattern was picked up on the facing interior walls. Larger rosettes were inlaid in the high, parquet ceiling. The floor matched that, but without the rosettes.

Groups of Western furniture formed sitting areas around the room, and Western art and pictures of the ranch in older days hung on the interior walls.

Dane approached one of the outside walls and ran his fingers softly along a fluted column. "This is really, really fine work."

"It's been featured in a couple of magazines over the years. Come on, Uncle Karl's office is this way."

I led him down a wide, carpeted hallway, past the playroom and the library to my uncle's office.

Uncle Karl sat at the huge desk both his father and grandfather had used, a pile of papers in front of him and the oversized computer screen to his left running a spreadsheet program. His cowboy hat was tipped back on his well-lined forehead, and he was rubbing his eyes when we walked in.

"Is that a good sign or bad?"

He looked up and gave me his classic "glad to see you" smile. It lit up his whole face, clear to his eyes.

He was a tall man, with just a tiny bit of a stomach on him and a head of thick, wavy brown hair now peppered with gray. He held a lot of authority with a loose hand, letting his born sense of fairness govern his decisions. But folks who knew him also knew not to cross him. His anger could match the force of a stampede, with none of the chaos.

"Good. We're doing real good, Josh." He nodded at Dane and rose. "Who's this?"

I made introductions, and they shook hands. Dane was as tall as my uncle, and standing just as straight and confidently.

"Proud to meet you. Jesse says you're planning to stay awhile?"

"If you can find me a place, sir."

"Son, even if we couldn't, you'd be welcome as long as you want to stay. Jesse mentioned you plenty in his messages from Afghanistan and Iraq, and we owe you an unpayable debt. That means something to me."

Dane nodded, but didn't move to brag or take advantage.

"Jesse also says you're good with tools?"

"Yes, sir. Been building and repairing wooden structures and furniture most of my life."

"Well, we got plenty of those kind of jobs on a place this big," Uncle Karl said. "We say good-bye to guests tomorrow morning, which means we have till Sunday afternoon to fix cabin problems. We've got a bad step on cabin one and a bad window sash on four. See what you can get done in that time, and then we'll talk about the door on the calving barn. Maybe you can start on that on Monday."

Uncle Karl opened a drawer and put some files away, then looked up at Dane again.

"You'll get the same pay as the summer hands, paid each Friday, plus a room with Jesse. You can eat with the hands or with Jesse and Josh, or with the guests when Jesse or Josh do. That sound fair?"

"Yes, sir, more than fair. Thank you."

"Glad to have you with us. You need anything, come see me, or ask Jesse or Josh. What you doing this afternoon?"

"Dane volunteered to help Sarah and me with the trail ride."

"Good. You're going to need it. You've got fourteen kids, mainly under twelve. And Steve Sanderson really wants to go with you. Can you manage that?"

"We can now that Dane's along. I was going to take Coyote Hill Trail."

He nodded. "Keep an eye on the sky. Make sure they all have rain gear, and be prepared to turn around if it looks threatening. Better to shorten the ride than get caught in a storm and deal with a bunch of worried parents."

"Yes, sir. Will do."

We headed back to the kitchen, where we wolfed down a quick lunch. Then Dane headed back to the barn, and I went into the dining room to touch base with Sarah.

"We're going over to the corral," I told her, coming to stand behind where she was eating at a table filled with little kids. "You bring the crew out when you're done, and we'll be ready. We can take Steve with no problem. You'll lead. Dane will take the middle, and I'll bring up the rear. Oh, and tell all the kids to bring raincoats."

She nodded, then turned and leaned into me. "Brittany's coming," she whispered. I nodded and headed outside.

Crap. That girl was sixteen going on thirty-five and boy crazy—with me getting all the attention. She'd been too close around me all week. Always touching my arm, asking me to help her mount up, offering to help me in the barn. She'd been like that last summer too. But she'd be leaving tomorrow, I reminded myself.

"Who's Steve Sanderson?" Dane asked when I got back to the barn.

"A great kid. Fourteen. He has cerebral palsy, and he's in a wheelchair. His arms don't work the best either, and he can't always speak clearly, but you can understand him if you listen. He's been coming here with his family for four years because we'll take him riding. Other places won't, I guess."

I took down a couple of the saddles we'd be using. "If you'll help me get him up in front of Sarah on her horse, I think we can manage with no problems."

"Probably be better if he rode in front of me," Dane offered.

"You okay with that?"

"Absolutely."

We'd barely finished checking saddles when the kids swarmed out of the big house. Sarah pushed Steve's wheelchair in front, leading like she was the Pied Piper. I did a quick scan for raincoats. Things seemed okay.

"Get ready for three hours of noise and chaos." I gave a loud whistle, and the kids quieted down. "Everybody, this is Dane."

"Hey, Dane," came the reply.

Then one of the little guys asked, "Where's your cowboy boots and hat, Dane?"

Dane looked down at his combat boots, then at the boy who had asked the question.

"What's your name?" he asked his inquisitor.

"I'm Jake," the towhead responded, pushing his cowboy hat back a bit on his head and sliding his wire-framed glasses up his nose. The top of Jake's hat barely reached Dane's belt buckle.

"Well, Jake," Dane answered, squatting down to the boy's size, "I've got a baseball cap in my pack. I guess I should put it on, hmm?"

"Yes, sir," Jake said, sounding very serious. "You don't want to get sunburned. Moms get mad at you."

"They do, don't they?" Dane said. "These are my special boots. I've worn them everywhere, and they've kept me out of trouble. But I suppose I will need cowboy boots one of these days, huh?"

"You should get them," Jake answered, as sure of himself as he could be. If I remembered right, he was from Chicago, and he was proudly wearing his very first pair of cowboy boots.

"You remember what I told you about cowboy hats, Jake?"

"Yes, Josh. 'Tie 'em tight under your chin. It's bad for a cowboy to have to chase his hat across the field.' And it's windy today, isn't it, Josh?"

"Sure is, Jake…." I waited a beat, and half the kids joined us in the next line. "It's always windy in Paradise Valley."

Dane crooked an eyebrow at me, and I shrugged. He'd find out soon enough.

Dane turned back to Jake. "So, pardner, would you like a little boost to get on your horse?"

I pointed Dane toward one of the smaller horses, and Dane, Sarah, and I began helping kids mount. I could hear Brittany telling Sarah that I'd help her, and I gritted my teeth. It's not that she was heavy. She was cute, blond, curvy, and used to getting her way.

Then I spotted Steve waiting patiently in his wheelchair, and I let the frustration go.

I helped Brittany up—she made sure it took two tries—and handed her the reins as she gushed her thanks and touched my arm.

"You bet, Brittany."

Then I turned to Steve and rolled his wheelchair up to Sugarpie. "Hey, Steve, we're going to put you in front of Dane on Sugarpie today, okay?"

"Dane," Steve repeated. "Sugarpie."

"That's right," Dane said as he held out his hand to shake Steve's. Steve waved his arm wildly, trying to line it up with Dane's. Dane smoothly grabbed his hand and shook it.

"Nice to meet you, Steve."

"Dane," Steve repeated.

Dane put Steve's raincoat in his pack, then mounted.

"Josh, you and Sarah move the wheelchair so the back is parallel with Sugarpie. Then just lift Steve to standing, and I'll do the rest," he instructed.

We did as directed. I was trying to figure how we'd lift Steve when Dane just reached down, grasped him gently under the arms, and dead-lifted him onto the saddle. With another smooth move, he lifted Steve's leg over the saddle, and the two of them were ready to go.

"Yeah!" Steve exulted, turning his head so he could look in Dane's direction.

"You liked that, huh?" Dane asked. Looking down at Steve, he smiled a smile that reached his eyes. For a second, I was jealous.

I pushed the chair into the barn and whistled at Hector. He lined himself up about ten feet in front of me. I took four running steps and vaulted onto his back. The kids cheered.

"Yeah, Josh!" Steve yelled.

I grinned and looked at Dane. He had the nerve to roll his eyes.

"All right, cowboys and cowgirls," I said, waving my hat. "You all follow Sarah now. Dane, you and Steve fall in the middle, and I'll take the rear. Let's get riding!"

Brittany ended up right in front of me, of course, and made a point of wiggling her butt in the saddle off and on. Her pants sat low, her shirt was cropped, and I could see her butterfly tattoo above her thong. Sometimes I did feel sorry for her, going to all that work and thinking I was interested.

As soon as we cleared the barns and corrals, the trail began to climb the open hillside. As we moved along, Sarah pointed out the flowers and trees, and the kids repeated the names to each other until the words made their way back to me.

Sarah was great with kids, maybe because she was so short. Or maybe the kids immediately sensed the understanding and acceptance she offered everyone. She never panicked either. I was always glad when she could help me on the rides.

Soon enough, we were into the pine woods and maneuvering the switchbacks that would get us over the ridge. From there, we'd cross a creek and drop down into a pretty meadow.

Sarah led at a good pace. Whenever we made a turn, I'd check how all the kids were sitting. All along the way, I could see Dane listening to whatever Steve said and occasionally making a comment himself. I'd have liked to hear the two of them, but I was stuck talking to Brittany.

"I wish I could just stay here, Josh."

"I think you'd get bored here, Brittany. The nearest mall is ninety minutes away. The nearest theater is in Livingston, and it shows only two movies at a time. And the Internet is slow. You wouldn't have much to do."

"But what do you do, Josh?"

"Me? I work the horses, cook and read, watch ball games on TV. Nothing exciting."

"Have you read any of *The Vampire Diaries*? That's my favorite series. I think it's better than *Twilight*."

"Nah, sorry. I mainly read horse magazines."

"Oh." She was quiet a minute. "Do you spend time with your girlfriend?"

"No time for a girlfriend. Hey, you hang back here. I'm going to ride up for a minute and make sure everybody is fine going across the creek."

Nobody had trouble with the creek, and pretty soon I was back with Brittany.

"You'd make time for me, though, wouldn't you, Josh?"

"So how's your family getting home tomorrow, Brittany? You flying out of Bozeman to LA, or are you going to head into Yellowstone for a few days first?"

"Yellowstone," she grimaced. "My dumb brother talked my folks into going out with a guide to look for wolves. I really don't want to."

"But that should be fun. You might even see some of the pups. It's that time of year."

"Who cares? I'd rather stay with you." She batted her eyes at me. "I'm sure we'd find something fun to do."

Crap.

"About the most fun thing I got coming up this weekend is picking up some new horse gear in Bozeman," I answered. "You wouldn't like it, really."

Luckily, she fell silent for a while, and Hector fell behind her mount as the trail dipped slightly. The trees were thinner here, and when I looked up, I could see the sky was dark gray now. The wind was picking up too.

In front of us, the meadow was a mass of high grass and wildflowers. Sarah had pulled up, the kids' mounts scattered around her. A few of the mares, and even some of the kids, eyed the sky nervously.

Not Brittany. She slid off her mount and began to wander among patches of yellow mule's ear and red paintbrush.

"Okay, everybody, how about we take a minute and get our raincoats on, and then we'll head back to the ranch for a snack?" I pulled my raincoat out of my saddlebag to set the example.

Dutifully, the kids put on their coats. Dane helped Steve into his.

"Brittany, get your coat on and mount up again so we can get moving."

"It's not going to rain, Josh. Let's get down and walk for a bit. Aren't the flowers pretty?"

Thunder rumbled.

"Come on, Brittany. It is going to rain. We need to get everybody back. Mount up."

"No. It's not going to rain."

Like that, the sky opened up.

"Brittany."

She just stared at me, batting her eyes against the downpour.

"It'll stop in a minute," she insisted. "Come on. Let's pick some flowers."

Lightning cracked across the sky, followed immediately by booming thunder. The rain came down harder, landing like sharp pin pricks on my coat before bouncing off.

A couple of the littler kids whimpered or called out for Sarah, who rode among them tightening their rain hoods. Two or three of the older kids joined me in urging Brittany to get back on her horse. But she kept up her little walk among the flowers, head down, not looking up at any of us.

It crossed my mind to dismount and throw her over the saddle, but Uncle Karl was adamant that Jesse and I never touch girl guests. I knew I couldn't leave Brittany here, and I couldn't stay here alone with her. I wasn't coming up with any good options.

Dane, I noticed, was eyeing everybody and everything over and over. Me, the kids, Brittany, the sky. His eyes kept moving, assessing, darting back and forth. Jeez, that'd make everybody more nervous if they noticed.

Before I could approach him to say something, he edged Sugarpie between the O'Brien twins, who were about twelve. He said something to them, then to Steve. Then he gently laid Steve over Sugarpie's neck and moved Steve's hands to grip her mane. One of the twins put her hand on Steve's back, and Dane dismounted. The other twin moved her horse closer and likewise put her hand on Steve.

Sure that Steve was secure, Dane marched for Brittany. He removed his raincoat and, in a series of quick moves that took her by surprise, wrapped it around her, picked her up, and heaved her on her mount.

She cried out in surprise as he thrust the reins in her hands, looked in her face, and said something I couldn't hear. She shrank back some and opened her mouth to reply, but Dane was already walking away. She was not happy.

"Let's get moving," Sarah called calmly, and the kids moved their horses into line behind her.

Already, Dane was back on Sugarpie, holding Steve upright in his arms. He looked at me, nodded, and nudged Sugarpie forward, following the line of horses now heading out of the meadow.

I felt about as tall as Jake, and dumber. Some leader I was. No way that would be attractive to Mr. Take Command.

Quick enough, we were back in the woods but not really out of the storm. The rain was relentless, reaching us through the tree cover. Lightning and thunder erupted every few minutes, and some of the littler ones started to cry.

"Hey now," Sarah called over her shoulder. "We're all okay. Who knows the words to 'She'll Be Coming Round the Mountain'? Let's sing."

Sarah really can't sing, but the older kids somehow found her nonexistent key and joined in. When we reached the verse about the six white horses, our horses picked up speed. I think they realized we were headed back to the dry barn.

Sarah made up a few verses after that. I rode back and forth along the line, checking everybody out but staying clear of Brittany. Her horse kept moving, and she stared straight ahead. Each of the older kids had picked up a younger buddy, and everybody was doing fine. The crying stopped.

Dane had to be freezing. His T-shirt was soaked, and I could see goose bumps all over his bare arms. But he sang along loudly, often messing up the lyrics so Steve laughed at him. Other kids began to laugh too.

"Isn't this a great adventure?" Sarah called out. If I was lucky, all the kids would repeat that line to their parents and forget about how frightened they'd been. Already I was dreading what Uncle Karl was going to say once we got back.

When we came in view of the big house, I could see most of the parents gathered in the great hall watching for us. Sarah aimed the line for the deck.

The sliding glass door flew open, and Aunt Kate called out, "Come on in here, you cowboys and cowgirls, and get some hot chocolate and sugar cookies."

The kids helped each other dismount and streaked for the door, Brittany among them. Dane was already carrying Steve inside.

By the time I reached the deck, everybody was in. Crisis averted. I did not look up to see if my uncle was watching. I grabbed Sugarpie's reins and Hector's, and I led them toward the barn. The other horses followed.

I was halfway through getting saddles off the mounts when I realized I wasn't the only human in the barn.

"I thought I told you to turn around at the big meadow." Uncle Karl's voice reached me before he came into view. Dane trailed behind him, wearing a dry shirt now and carrying a towel and a thermos.

"I tried, Uncle Karl." Crap, I sounded like a whiner.

"You tried?" he shot back. He stood close by me now, his legs planted wide, his arms folded across his chest, staring at me.

"Do you know the handful of trouble your aunt had keeping those parents calm? What kept you from turning those kids around?" He spoke louder with each sentence, and I tried to find a place to look at that didn't include his unhappy face.

"Uncle Karl, honestly, Brittany wouldn't get back on her horse, and I couldn't figure out what to do short of throwing her on it. And I knew I couldn't do that—"

"And I threw her on her horse, sir," Dane finished. "Josh tried to reason with her, but she wasn't cooperating. Better to injure her pride than endanger the others."

Uncle Karl turned to look at him now, and Dane returned his stare.

"You didn't swear, did you?"

"No, sir."

"At least you've got more restraint than Jesse."

"I got more of a lot of things than Jesse," Dane answered.

Uncle Karl threw back his head and laughed. "I believe you do." He grabbed the thermos from Dane and handed it to me. "Here. Your aunt thought you'd be cold. Have some hot chocolate. I know that girl is a problem."

Dane tossed the towel over my shoulder. Then he and Uncle Karl began to help me with the horses.

Jesse came in as we were finishing up, and he was grinning big, making those dimples all the girls loved look like canyons in his cheeks.

"I hear Brittany gave you a hard time, little brother."

"Not in the mood."

"Aw, what's the matter? Don't you like a little attention from the girls now and then?"

I really wanted to smack the grin off his face.

Uncle Karl interrupted the fight before it could go anywhere. He'd been doing it all our lives. "Why don't you two take the rest of the day off? Take Dane to Cunningham's."

Assuming Jesse would pitch in now and we would follow his orders, Uncle Karl strode out of the barn.

Cunningham's was the nearest bar, alongside the Yellowstone River just beyond the blinking light that let drivers on Highway 89 know they'd reached the crossroads that was Emigrant. The town had about 370 residents scattered around a combination gas station/grocery, a fly-fishing outfitter, town hall, bank, post office, church, bakery, café, and a pair of bars.

"That's a great idea," Jesse said. "Let's leave in an hour. Josh, you invite Sarah, and we'll meet you there."

Great. I'd get to spend the evening with Dane. I'd have a hard-on, and he'd be looking at me like I was an idiot who couldn't handle a teenaged girl.

THREE

BY THE time I reached Cunningham's, Jesse, Dane, and Sarah were there. Sarah had changed into tighter jeans, a frilly white shirt, and a snug, spangled denim vest that showed off her well-rounded figure. Her blond hair hung loose past her shoulders.

I noticed Ray Hanson and his hands sitting at the bar and sighed. No way I could just walk past them.

"Well, if it ain't the great horse whisperer," Ray said loud enough for everyone around to hear. "That new horse of yours throw you yet?" His buddies laughed, overly loud I thought.

"Nope. Doing fine, Ray." I wanted to keep moving, but he grabbed my arm.

"Come on, Brooks, tell us how you're doing. You need help?"

He seemed interested, but he was also more than a little drunk. I was cautious. He hadn't let go of my arm yet either.

"That horse is a difficult one," I offered, removing his hand from mine at the same time. I wanted to spare his pride, but I wanted to get away from him. "I got folks waiting on me, Ray."

"Yeah, yeah, go on," he mumbled. "I'll come by one day and see how you're doing."

I bit my lip to keep from saying anything and moved on. Hanson ordered another beer.

"Here's your beer, Josh." Ben Cunningham slid a PBR my way. "You sure I can't persuade you to come work for me instead of your uncle?" He'd been asking me for two months now.

"Who you got in the kitchen today?" Poor Ben. He was a good guy, my age. He'd run the bar with his mom for years. He cooked until he was old enough to tend bar. Then they swapped places. Since her death, he couldn't find a good cook.

"Sally Jensen. No special tonight. It, ah, didn't turn out. You're okay as long as you order a hamburger."

"Thanks for the advice." I raised my beer to Ben and headed to our table.

"We already ordered for you," Jesse said as I sat down. "What did Hanson want?"

"He wants to help me with Hurricane."

"Like hell," Jesse snapped. "Do not have anything to do with that man."

"Yes, Jesse."

"I'm serious, Josh." Jesse banged his index finger into the table to make his point. "That man is trying to create a real feud between you two, one that'll have the whole valley choosing him as the better horse trainer if he has his way. Stay away from him."

"I know, Jesse." I sighed. I was not the little brother who didn't understand things anymore, didn't he see that?

"We ordered a hamburger for you," Sarah offered. "Did Ben ask you to work for him again?" It was her way of changing the topic, and I was grateful.

"He did." I took a drink of my beer and nodded at her. "You think I should take him up on the offer now?"

"You do and I will—"

"Hah! Gotcha, Jesse." Sarah was all smiles as she bounced triumphant in her seat.

Jesse grimaced at her, but it quickly turned to a grin. They stared each other down a long time before laughing and turning back to their beers. Too long, I thought. I cast a sideways glance at Dane, but he seemed amused.

Sally Jensen arrived with our burgers, and we all began to eat, avoiding any mention that the beef was burned. Somebody started the jukebox, a slow oldie by George Strait. Sarah loved to dance. I stood up and held out my hand.

"Come on, pardner."

She popped out of her chair and sashayed ahead of me onto the small dance floor. Once I had her in my arms, though, she was quiet for a while.

"What's up?"

She leaned back and looked up at me. "What do you think of Dane?"

"I was hoping he was my type. Why?"

"He makes me uneasy."

"Because?"

"There's a lot of... I don't know... something in that man. Darkness, anger, maybe sadness, all rolled together. He's wound real tight."

"Sarah, give him a break. He's just quit the Army, and he's been in Afghanistan pretty much nonstop for a few years."

"Do you really think he's your type?" She stopped moving her feet as she said this, and I almost stumbled. "You do, and you really are interested in him, aren't you?" She frowned and searched my face. "Josh, please promise me you'll be careful."

"Sarah, honestly, don't worry. It's not like he's going to hurt me or anything."

"Not physically."

"Sarah, nothing's happening. And I don't even know yet if anything might."

She had been my best friend and protector since kindergarten, from the day she told me she had a crush on Timmy Benson and I told her I did too. She had put her little index finger to my lips and told me not to tell another person, and she'd kept my secret ever since. Plenty of folks in the valley thought we'd be getting married. It protected me, and Sarah seemed not to mind that no one asked her out.

When the next song ended, I headed for the bar to get us each another beer. She went back to our table. Dane got up as she approached and held out her chair for her. Once they both sat down, he cast several sidelong glances at her, like he was trying to figure things out. Crap.

I returned with two beers and passed one off to Sarah. She immediately clinked it with mine.

"Here's to getting your week with Brittany over before the beginning of August this year," she said.

I smiled. "The rest of the summer is looking good."

After a pause, I turned to Dane. "Thanks for getting us all going again."

There, I'd broached the awful subject. I hoped Dane wouldn't be too hard on me. Talk about being a wimp.

He nodded. "Sorry I didn't know the rule. But I would have broken it anyway. We had to get out of there."

"It was a good move," Sarah agreed, "and you're the only one who could do it. Brittany would have had Uncle Karl after Josh if he'd done it. She's a wily one, that girl."

"Girls seem to like you, Josh," Dane said.

Crap. I leaned back in my seat, hoping to hide my face in the shadows or fall through some hole in the floor.

"It's not his fault," Sarah said, coming to my defense. "It's just that he's the only approachable Brooks male under sixty. Jesse is always out with the cattle, so girls can't meet him." She slapped my brother's arm playfully, and he grinned.

Poor Sarah. She was defending me without even realizing she was one of the girls Dane was talking about.

"Sarah, you wanna dance?" It was Jesse. He'd begun asking her around the Fourth of July and hadn't stopped. It made me nervous every time. I couldn't stand to think about those two getting close. So far, Sarah had always said no.

"Sorry, Jesse." She lowered her head and studied her beer. Suddenly, she looked sad. "I think that cold ride tired me out more than I knew. I'm going to have to call it a night."

We all stood up as she did. She shot me a look I couldn't read. Was she angry? About Dane still? Then she waved and headed for the door.

When we sat down again, we each began glancing round the bar in different directions. Dane watched the crowd, and I wondered if the crowd and the noise were getting to him. Jesse had been sensitive to it when he first got out of the Rangers.

I eyed Hanson and his buddies. A line of beer bottles stretched in front of each of them now, and they were louder than when I'd come in. Jesse studied the ladies. I could see the moment he made his decision.

"See you, boys," he said as he stood. He made his way to the corner booth where Carrie Kilbourne and Jane Martin were. I figured he was interested in Jane.

"So, what's Sarah got against Jesse?" Dane asked.

"Nothing." Jeez, what to say when there was so much I didn't want to let on. What kind of brother would he think I was if he found out I didn't want Jesse to date my best friend? "Jesse's suddenly interested. Sarah's not."

"You think she's not?" Dane arched an eyebrow at me.

"Definitely."

I didn't want to see him shake his head, so I looked around again, hoping there was an empty pool table. No such luck.

"You want another beer?"

"Still got half left."

The jukebox started playing Brooks and Dunn's "Nothing About You," and we both watched Jesse lead Jane onto the dance floor.

"Looks like your brother is making headway on Plan B."

"Yeah. Looks like you'll be riding home with me."

Dane didn't say anything, and we drank without talking for a while.

"So did you spend more time in Iraq or Afghanistan?" I asked, trying to think up something to say.

"Once I picked up Pashto, it was mainly Afghanistan," he answered. "But let's stay off that subject."

"Sorry." Maybe it was something only he and Jesse could talk about. What'd I know since I hadn't been there? I kept my mouth shut so he could pick the next topic. But he stayed quiet. He didn't seem uneasy with it, and he sure wasn't worried that I might be.

I kept a steady eye on the various corners of the bar, watching Hanson and his buddies, and Jesse talking with Jane. Every once in a while, in the kitchen, a plate crashed to the floor. Behind the bar, Ben would wince. He was keeping count.

Finally, Dane started talking again. "So, what time do you think I can get into those cabins your uncle wants me to work on?"

"By eleven, I'm guessing. There'll be breakfast at eight thirty, and then a lot of good-byes. I'll need to be up there for that. And then families loading up their cars. I help with suitcases and stuff. Yeah, I'd say eleven."

"You want another beer?"

"Nah. But you go ahead."

Dane shook his head. "I'm game to go if you are, cowboy."

I left money on the table, and we got up. As we walked out, Jesse smiled and waved.

"SORRY. My radio's busted," I said once we got in the truck.

Dane seemed to take up all the room inside, and I suddenly had to concentrate to get the truck out of the parking lot. All my senses wanted to do was focus on him, the energy vibrating off him, his smell, and the moonlight moving across the sharp planes of his face. Dane didn't say anything. He just looked out the window. The silence crawled up my skin like an itch.

"You know, you might want to spend the night at my place."

He didn't answer. Okay. Well, maybe this was going nowhere. Maybe that was a good thing. At least I wouldn't make a fool of myself. I was so caught up in my own internal conversation I didn't realize Dane was talking until he'd finished.

"What?"

He turned to look at me. "I said, I think I will sleep with you tonight, cowboy."

"You'll be glad you did." Crap, didn't that sound sleazy and stupid. "I mean, Jesse tends to use up a lot of the house when he brings home a girl, if you know what I mean."

I tried to smile, but my face froze when I looked at Dane. He was watching my lips like they were dinner and he hadn't eaten in a month. Slowly, he licked his own. My cock jumped, and I jerked my gaze back toward the road in self-preservation.

"And how are you when you bring home a new guy?"

"Uh, yeah, well...."

"Relax, cowboy." Dane dropped his hand on my thigh. "Just relax."

I tried. But my thigh burned where he touched me, and I thought my swollen cock might rip through my jeans any second. *Eyes on the road, eyes on the road.* My hands got sweaty on the wheel, and the tires spun and gravel flew when I turned off the highway onto the dirt road to the ranch. Dane chuckled. I didn't dare look at him.

Once we passed the big house, I picked up speed all the way to my place. Then I threw the truck in park and killed the engine.

"All right," I said stupidly.

Dane opened his door and slowly unfolded himself from the cab. I jumped out and led the way toward the cabin.

Inside, I watched him make a study of my living room. The furniture was leftover from when Gran had lived here: her upholstered couch and afghan, her leather chairs and doilies, her wood stove and ceiling fan. The only things I'd added were a flat-screen TV and a solid, wooden coffee table, and I replaced her embroidered flower pictures with photographs of horses. Doorways from this room led to the kitchen and to the hallway where the bedroom and bathroom were. What was he thinking?

"You want anything to eat or drink?"

"No, thanks. I'm good."

My heart pounded, loud enough I was sure Dane could hear it. "You want—"

Without warning he grabbed me around my neck with one huge hand and threw me up against the front door. My hat tumbled to the floor. I was having trouble breathing, and all he was doing was pressing his thumb under my jaw. With his other hand, he grabbed my crotch and slammed my ass against the door too.

I made myself go perfectly still. He didn't let up any, but I could tell he'd noticed and seemed pleased.

"Now, cowboy," he said slowly, "tell me what your game is. You come on to me in the barn and in your truck, but you dance with Sarah like she means something to you."

He moved his thumb a hair so I could get enough breath to answer.

"You jerk—"

Just like that, the pressure was back on.

"Okay," I rasped. I was not going to gasp out an excuse and sound like a pansy. I waited. I couldn't breathe and my heart pounded, but I made myself stay still. I knew he wasn't going to kill me.

The pressure let up once more, and I took in a controlled breath.

"Sarah has been my friend forever. My *best* friend. But I sleep with guys. You don't want to, I'll take the couch. It's up to you."

He loosened his grip on my neck, but not on my crotch. And he kept staring at me. I twisted my neck left, then right, then stared back. It took all the courage I had not to look away, but I knew somewhere deep inside that I'd lose something real important if I did.

He rested his right hand loosely on my shoulder, his thumb stroking my collarbone, and ground his left against my zipper. I moaned and thrust into his hand, then grabbed onto a huge bicep to steady myself. Hot pressure built in my balls and cock.

"Dane, please…."

"Quiet," he snapped. He moved his right hand to my waist. "You stay quiet and do as I say. Open your eyes."

I hadn't realized I'd closed them. He still stared at me intently. He moved his right hand again, down my side to rest on my hip, and his eyes followed, sweeping from my head to my crotch, then staying where they stopped.

"You are a good-looking thing, cowboy."

"I wanna see more of your muscles."

He squeezed my hip hard. "I said quiet."

I gulped and nodded.

"Off with the shirt."

His order came out with a growl, and he moved back one step to give me room to obey. I tore my shirt out of my pants and worked the buttons with fumbling fingers. When I'd undone the last one, I looked at him again. His jaw hardened.

"I said off."

I took it off. I didn't look as buff as he did, but I wasn't embarrassed. Muscling horses and throwing hay bales is a good workout. He looked me over for another long minute, then moved in and swiped his tongue across one of my nipples. It went hard and goose bumpy all at once. I put my hands on his head to keep him there.

"Hands above your head," he snapped. "I'll do the touching."

"Do you want me to say yes, sir too?"

I gasped and my arms flew above my head when he squeezed my balls hard.

"Okay, okay."

He squeezed again, gentler this time, and tongued all around my nipple. I had to remind myself to keep my hands above my head. The position made me feel stupid, but soon enough I forgot that. He was more than arousing me. I whimpered, then squirmed like a kid who had to pee. I wanted him to lick me everywhere. I wanted to touch him. My Wranglers were so tight I started thinking they wouldn't come off or, worse, that I might come in them.

"Dane, please."

He stepped back, smiling at my discomfort. His eyes blazed hot. Otherwise, he didn't look bothered.

"Take off the boots and jeans."

I managed the boots with a few hops. The pants and briefs were an undignified struggle.

"You know, we could go find a bed." I was standing naked against my front door, my cock red and stiff as a fence pole, while he still had all his clothes on. It was embarrassing. But then I saw the bulge in his jeans and smiled.

He stepped toward me again and ran a hand down my jaw. "Yeah, cowboy, you be proud," he teased.

His mouth fell on mine, his tongue pushing inside, deep in my throat, running along my teeth, teasing along my tongue. He smelled woodsy and tasted sweet and beery. His stubble scratched my face, and the tingle made my cock throb. I relaxed and let him do whatever he wanted.

I brought my hands to rest on his waist, and I burrowed under his shirt to feel skin. Wherever I touched, he had muscles. Hard, smooth, powerful. I slid my hands lower to feel his ass. More muscles, flexing now as he pumped and rubbed his denim-packed cock against my bare one. The touch of the scratchy fabric made mine weep. I squeezed a handful of his ass. It was like grabbing steel. I moaned.

"You. Naked. Now," I mumbled, frantically working his belt buckle.

He froze. "What did I say you were supposed to do?"

My hands began to tremble.

"N-nothing. Not talk."

"And are you doing it?"

"Sorry, sorry."

He ran a finger down my cheek. His lips whispered across mine. "Now, do as I say."

I nodded.

He smiled. "Don't move."

He dropped to his knees and flicked his tongue across me. I thought I was gonna die. It had been so long. I fell back against the door, and he grabbed my waist and held me up.

"Hands behind your head."

He looked up to make sure I did it, then lowered his mouth to my cock again.

"Mmmm," he moaned, the sound vibrating down to my balls. My prick jumped like it had a life of its own.

His tongue was all over me, licking up the front, twirling around the head, pushing into the slit. He nipped me all the way back down, then sucked one of my balls into his mouth. A shiver like electricity shot through me. I squirmed some more and slammed my arms into the door to keep from grabbing his hair, afraid he'd stop if I did.

When he began to do everything all over again, I had to push him away from me.

"Stop or I'll come."

He ignored me and continued his tongue's wicked assault.

A growl punched through my clenched teeth as I exploded, long spurts shooting down his throat. He groaned and kept swallowing and sucking and holding me up.

When I was aware of myself again, he was kissing up and down my cock, whispering, "Good, so good."

I played my fingers through his coarse hair, petting him, and he rubbed his stubbly chin across my stomach. I made to slide down to my knees, and he sat back on his heels to let me. I started working his shirt buttons.

"You now. I want to see and touch you."

He held his arms out so I could remove his shirt. The yellow porch light streaming in the door window was all I had to see by, but it was enough. He was beautiful.

He watched as I moved my hands slowly over his chest and down his chiseled abs. To my calloused fingers, his skin felt smooth, the muscles underneath rock hard. I stopped when I hit a rough patch on his right side. It was large, and I retraced it.

"Roadside bomb," he said.

I looked up in surprise. He was staring into the dark, like he was seeing something far away. Then he blinked and cocked his head.

"Keep going."

He let me push him down to the floor. I crawled up his legs, sat on his thighs, and kept exploring, and he let me. Soon I found another, smaller punctuation of scar tissue.

"Bullet."

Pictures of what he must have been through flooded my mind, images from every war movie I'd ever seen. Explosions, bursts of gunfire. I closed my eyes to stop them.

"Don't think about it. Keep going." I felt his hands warm on mine, urging me to move them again.

When I did, he dropped his hands to his zipper and undid it. I eased his jeans down his hips, sliding my hands down muscled thighs and more scars. Jeez, how many did he have?

But I didn't go there. I concentrated on his hard, flat stomach. I began kissing my way to the coarse dark hair that made a neat mat below his belly button. My chin bumped into his cock, and it jerked. Like him, it was big and powerful. I ran my fingers up and down it once, twice.

"Yes." I don't know which of us said it.

I closed my fist around the wide base and took his tip between my lips, mouthing it like the top of an ice cream cone I wanted a bite of. He groaned and pumped his hips, and I smiled. It was power like you had over a horse, having this effect on a man.

He smelled of musk, and I inhaled deeply. I kept pumping and licking and sucking him. I got lost in it, moving against the smooth skin, tasting the bitterness of his precum until his hands pulled me off him.

"I want to fuck your ass, cowboy. Where's the supplies?"

"Bedroom."

He pulled me up and pushed me down the hall, following right behind. A hard swat fell across my butt.

"Hey!" It stung and made me hard both.

"What you going to do about it?"

He laughed, and God, it sounded good. I wanted to make him laugh for days. Then maybe he'd forget what had caused the scars and made his eyes so scary.

I led the way into my room and opened the nightstand next to the bed. I'd just managed to grab the lube and some condoms when he heaved me up and set me on all fours on the bed like I weighed no more than Steve Sanderson.

"Pretty," he sighed. "Stay that way, cowboy. No, wait. I think I'll have some of this first."

He spread my ass and licked down my crack. I groaned.

"Oh, man, this is going to be the best night of my life." It came out before I could stop it.

He laughed, and I realized how dumb I was.

"Crap." I dipped my head to the bedspread and covered it with my arms.

"That's kind of cute."

"Cute?" I started to crawl across the bed, trying to flee to someplace to hide my embarrassment. He reached out and grabbed me.

"Oh, no. You stay right here for the best night of your life."

I felt one hand stroke my ass while the fingers of the other began to tease my hole. I shivered all over, and he laughed again. He punched a finger through and withdrew it. The pang of pain was followed by hollow emptiness.

"Dane… please."

"Please what, cowboy?"

He slipped his finger inside me deep, then stilled.

My gut jumped and I grasped at the sheets. "Dane." It was all I could manage to say.

He twisted his finger and curled it, scraping my prostate as he withdrew. I yelped and jumped, and he laughed again.

Then he probed my hole with two fingers, dipping in, stretching me, and withdrawing, repeating the pattern over and over, getting me ready. I groaned my pleasure.

"Mmmm," he answered.

Cool lube hit my crack, followed by the sound of the condom packet tearing. He spread me wide, and I felt his cock poke me and plunge in. The sharp pain burned, and I gasped. God, but he was big.

He stilled and began to rub soft, warm circles across my back.

"Tell me when," he breathed. "But don't make me wait too long. Fuck, cowboy, you feel good."

Heat spread through my insides, burning me everywhere in a good way, and I grinned like a fool.

"Okay. It's okay."

He moved, a gentle rocking that eased into slow, long pushes and pulls that lit up every nerve ending I had. When he sped up, his balls slapped my ass, and I bounced across the bed until I had to grip the headboard to keep from hitting the wall.

Groans and grunts and smells of sweat and sex filled the room. He grabbed my hips and pulled me up higher so every thrust hit my prostate. I yelped.

"Nice, isn't it?" His chuckle melted into grunts again.

I could barely manage a moan in reply. I was lost in a rush of intense sensations spiraling high toward a peak I wanted to throw myself off of.

"Oh yes, you are one nice, tight ass."

He reached around and grabbed me. I was hard again.

"Bet you could come again, couldn't you?"

"Yes." I thrust back and forth between his gripping fingers and the fat cock that impaled me. Then he began to thrust again and rub my dick fast and hard in the same rhythm.

"Now you do it," he ordered, gripping my hips hard with both hands and snapping his torso into my ass.

I shot as soon as I grabbed myself, shuddering hard and pumping strings of cum across my chest and stomach.

Dane thrust deep twice more and froze. Giving a strangled growl, he spurted hard into the condom, then collapsed across my back without warning, smashing me into the bed. His quick breaths tickled my ear.

Soon enough, he rolled to lie beside me on his back, his chest heaving up and down as he dragged in air.

"Bathroom?"

"Down the hall."

"Be back."

I didn't move. When he returned, he wiped a warm washcloth down my ass, then pulled the blanket at the bottom of the bed across me. He slipped in next to me to lie on his back, and I moved over against him, draping my arm across his stomach. He pulled me close with a hand that stayed possessively on my ass. I was crazy happy sated just listening to him breathe. Pretty soon, the evenness told me he was asleep.

"This was the best," I whispered when I knew he couldn't hear. But I should have known, worst follows best a lot of the time.

FOUR

I SLID out of bed early and went into the kitchen. I put on the coffee and started making blueberry pancakes and bacon. I thought the smell would lure Dane in, but he didn't appear, so I went back to the bedroom to check on him.

He was still asleep, but he was mumbling now, tense and agitated, sweat beaded across his face. I leaned over and touched his shoulder to wake him.

"Dane? Dane, breakfast is—"

He sprang at me with a startled cry and knocked me over. Before I could say anything more, we were both on the floor, him on top of me throwing painful punches to my gut.

"Dane! Dane, stop! It's Josh."

He looked down at me, a dazed expression on his face. He shook his head, then looked at me again.

"Fuck. Josh, what did you do? Oh, fuck."

He rolled off me and sat on the floor. I sat up and rubbed my stomach, working to catch my breath again.

"What happened?" I asked at last.

But Dane wasn't looking at me. He wore a terrible scowl, his jaw clenched tight. He seemed to be looking off somewhere far away. An instant later, he jerked his head, and he was back in the room. And he was mad.

"Don't ever do that to me," he yelled. "Fuck. Never mind. It won't happen again."

He rolled up onto his feet and headed for the door.

"What do you mean? What the heck happened here?"

"Nothing." He glanced at me and winced. "Fuck."

He rubbed his hand across his face, and he seemed surprised when he felt the sweat. He stared at his palm for a moment like he was trying to figure what to do about the wet; then he wiped his palm across his hip and stared at the floor, then the ceiling.

"Tell me what's going on, Dane. Whatever it is—"

"Let's just say I've come to my senses." He shook his head, still looking anywhere but at me.

"What's that supposed to mean?"

He took a deep breath. "Cowboy, your brother is my best friend. Probably my only friend. I don't know if he knows about you, but he sure as shit doesn't know about me, and I can't mess that up."

Then he was through the doorway and down the hall. He already had his pants and shirt on, and his boots were in his hand when I entered the living room.

"I'm sorry." His back was to me, and he threw the words over his shoulder as he opened the front door. He slammed it behind him like some final word as I crossed the room. I pulled it open again.

"Dane, wait a minute! Jane's probably still at Jesse's. I made breakfast. Come back."

But he didn't. He walked barefoot across the stone drive like it was smooth as sand, no hitch or halt to his step no matter what he stepped on. When he reached his truck, he threw the boots inside and followed them in, then slammed the door shut. He didn't look at me again.

I didn't go after him, afraid he'd make me feel way more foolish than he already had. I went back to the bedroom and got dressed, then left breakfast sitting in the pans and headed for the big house to help guests with their luggage. I took my truck so he couldn't watch me walk down the road. It was childish I suppose, but I felt like I was protecting myself, even if it was only my pride. Still, I chanced a glance in the direction of his truck. I couldn't see him, and I didn't know whether that meant he'd gone into Jesse's house or he was lying down on the front seat.

It wasn't until I had to dodge my first big puddle that I realized we must have had a serious storm overnight. Funny. I felt like I'd been rained on hard too.

I MADE pleasant comments when required and tried not to let on to guests that my gut was hurting. I just concentrated on hauling bags. Nothing I carried was heavier than the uneasiness I felt. I could not figure what had happened.

I had just loaded Brittany's two weighty suitcases into her parents' car when I heard someone coming up behind me. I spun around hoping it was Dane, but it was Brittany.

"Hey, you're all set. See you next year." It was the same mindless thing I'd said to everyone.

"You won't," she replied as she marched past me.

"Huh?"

"You won't see me next year." She opened the car door and got in. But she left the door open. "I've told my parents I'm not doing this vacation ever again."

"Aw, Brittany, come on. Nobody's blaming you for how the ride ended." She might be a difficult teen, but I didn't want her beating herself up about the trail ride. I remembered being her age and wanting to be noticed. "You just didn't want the fun to end. No one will even remember it next year."

"No next year," she repeated. "And, like I care anyway." She slammed the car door, hit the lock, and turned her back to me.

When Brittany hit the horn, I jumped. When her parents didn't hurry any, she hit it again. I moved off, looking around for more bags to haul.

That's when I spotted Dane on the walkway by the big house, squatting down to talk with Steve Sanderson. He listened for a long while, maybe said a few words. He stood up when Steve's mom walked up, and he spoke to her. Then he patted Steve on the shoulder, smiled, and walked away. Steve had a big grin on his face, and Mrs. Sanderson wiped her eye as they both watched him head for one of the empty cabins.

Obviously, he wasn't mad at everybody.

"Like I care anyway," I said to myself. The heck with him.

FIVE

ONCE the last guest was gone, I headed for the corral near my cabin, intent on spending time with Hurricane. Working with him would get my mind off things.

I grabbed a halter, blanket, and saddle and stepped into the corral. Hurricane turned toward me and walked right over. Ending things on a positive note the past two days was clearly paying off with him.

I spent a long time rubbing him with my hands and the rope, reminding him I was his friend. Then I slipped on the halter, and we went to work reviewing all we'd accomplished so far. By the time I had him switching from a walk to a lope and a canter and back down, he was licking his lips again in contentment.

God, he was beautiful. His black mane and tail fluttered behind him. His movements were controlled and powerful. He glistened. He made the blue sky behind him brighter because he was under it.

I stepped up to give him another good rubdown, and he nuzzled my shoulder.

"So you're going to turn into a lover on me, are you? And all because I treat you with kindness and firmness both? Tell me, would it work with a human, do you think?"

His snort wasn't much of an answer. I shouldn't have expected more.

"Okay. Let's try one more thing today."

I brought the blanket and saddle into his line of sight and set them down in the corral in a dry patch between mud puddles so he could check them out. When he'd sniffed them all he wanted, I took up the blanket and slowly put it on his back. I settled some of my upper body weight on it too, to get him used to what came next. When it was clear he was calm with it, I sat the saddle on his back.

This is where a horse can get really stuck. A trainer has to show the horse that he can still move his feet with a saddle on. Otherwise the horse has no place to go but up. As in bucking. Grabbing Hurricane's halter rope, I backed him up and then had him move toward me again until I could touch his back on his right side. Slowly, I let the saddle cinch down. Then I backed him up and moved him forward again, so I could touch his left side. I eased my hand down his middle, grabbed the cinch, threaded the billet strap through, and pulled it tight. He was wearing a saddle now, firmly on, and he hadn't snorted, bucked, or bitten me. Staying in place, using just the halter rope to guide him, I had him walk in a circle around me. Then I took off the rope.

"Now, boy, it's time for you to get used to the saddle."

I left the corral and watched him explore his new condition. He moved some, and the stirrups flapped and startled him like I knew they would. He jumped left and right, each movement getting him more used to the saddle's weight and the stirrups' movement. Eventually, he began to walk freely around the corral. Then I moved him to a pasture and left him alone for a couple hours to get to where that saddle felt as much a part of him as his tail was.

"Nice job, Josh," Jesse said as I walked past the barn. I hadn't realized he'd been watching.

"You think?"

"You're making fine progress."

"I need to."

"You had a lot to overcome."

"Yeah, Hanson. Why did he even bother to buy this horse?"

"Only Hanson knows." Jesse was quiet for a minute. Then he started in on another lecture. "I don't care if you have to lie, don't tell Hanson how you're doing. You understand me?"

Crap. Did he really think I couldn't manage this thing on my own? But I didn't want to get mad at him. I nodded and changed the subject.

"Jane gone?"

"Jane?"

"Yeah, Jane. The girl you brought home last night."

"Little brother, you gotta catch up. I haven't brought a girl home for a while now. I've changed my ways."

I didn't believe him for a minute. My brother loved girls, all girls. "And why would that be?"

"You'll see."

I knew it was all he was going to say. It was like when we were kids and he was so secretive he wouldn't tell me what he'd gotten Mom for Christmas.

"Later," he said and waved. "I'm heading out to check on the cattle behind your place."

IT WAS Saturday night, our one night without guests or kitchen and house help. Sarah, who stayed at the big house during the week because it was easier, had gone home to her apartment in Gardiner for the night.

Uncle Karl, Aunt Kate, and I had just sat down to dinner in the big house kitchen when Jesse and Dane came in. Dane was careful not to look at me directly, even when I passed him the potatoes and roast beef.

He and Jesse served themselves, and both ate several big forkfuls before Jesse began to talk.

"I found a downed fence along the national forest line behind Josh's house."

My gaze shot round the table. Jesse was calmly buttering a piece of bread. Uncle Karl was waiting to hear more. I'd been the last one to check that line.

"Jesse, that line was fine when I checked it in June."

Jesse nodded. "Fence is fixed. No cattle missing," he said between bites of the bread.

"What do you figure did it?" Uncle Karl asked.

"Not what. Who. Looks like a truck plowed it down to me."

"You're kidding? And whoever did it didn't bother to tell us?" Aunt Kate's thick, silver braid flew across her back as she spun her head first toward Jesse, then at Uncle Karl.

"Find any other clues?" he asked my brother.

"Truck tracks in the mud, and red paint scrapes on one of the downed posts."

"Mud? They were up there today?"

"I think so, Uncle Karl. Probably left just before I got there."

"Who'd have reason to be up there?" Dane asked.

"Could be anybody," Uncle Karl said. "That national forest access road is open to the public."

"It's posted with signs indicating the property beyond the road is private," Jesse explained. "Most people respect that."

"Were they after the cattle?" Dane asked.

"I suppose that's a possibility," Jesse said. "Everybody in the valley knows that's where part of our herd is this time of year. Only other things nearby are mine and Josh's places."

"This doesn't sound good," Aunt Kate said. She had quit eating and pushed her plate away. Now she was biting her lower lip and clasping and unclasping her hands.

Uncle Karl took one of them in his own, dwarfing it. Everything about Aunt Kate was petite. I forgot that sometimes because she was such a big presence in the running of the ranch.

"Kate, don't worry. It's probably just kids. Or a tourist who got stuck in the mud, took out the fence, and took off."

He turned to Jesse. "Still, you and the hands move the cattle to near Coyote Hill Trail tomorrow."

"On it," Jesse said. "I sent Eli and Ron up there to camp tonight. They've got radios and plenty of lights, and they're armed."

My brother looked to Aunt Kate to reassure her. "I don't think they'll have problems. I just want them to be extra careful. I'll check in on them too."

"Good." Uncle Karl nodded and looked round the table. "Even after the cattle are gone tomorrow, everybody keep an eye out. Josh, you ride up there a couple times a week when you're exercising horses. Not with guests, though. Jesse, you and the hands check it out on ATVs regular too. That should put an end to it if it's not over already."

He turned to my aunt again. "And Kate, don't worry. I think it's nothing. I'm just being careful."

He looked around the table at each of us. "We keep this among ourselves for now."

Dane and Jesse took off right after dinner. I helped Aunt Kate with the dishes, and we did what we could to get some things ready for the guests and the week ahead.

On the way home, when I went past Jesse's, I could hear through an open window that he and Dane were watching a baseball game and having a good time too.

I kept going, my mind wrapped up in images of Dane and me together, Dane grabbing me, touching me, fucking me, and ultimately pushing me away. Thinking it was all over already made my gut ache, and not from the punches he'd thrown.

SIX

JESSE took off early the next morning, and Dane avoided me by working on the guest cabins. I headed for Bozeman.

After getting the horse gear I needed, I drove to Main Street and the storefront where my college buddy, Guy, had his art gallery, studio, and apartment. He was my first lover and still a friend with benefits.

The gallery was closed, but I went around to the back door and knocked. After a while, the door opened a crack. Guy reached out and dragged me inside. Then he slammed the door behind us and locked it.

"You owe somebody money, Guy?" As if. His parents had left him a nice inheritance.

"No, silly. I just don't want someone to see me and demand that I open the gallery."

He giggled in the high-pitched way he'd had as long as I'd known him. Heck, he'd probably done it since he was a baby. He sounded gay, and I often wondered if it caused him problems as a kid. By college, when I met him, he was wide-open out. He didn't let anyone make an issue about that or the giggle, which was pretty amazing considering he was short. He was always upbeat and carefree. My aunt, when she met him, called him charmed.

"I was wondering when you were going to stop by again."

He gave me a fake shy smile and shoved me up the stairs toward his apartment, his hands lingering on my ass. I picked up the pace, and he moved his hands to grab my waist as he jogged up the steps behind me. I opened the door at the top, and we were in his kitchen, a sunny, blue room filled with gleaming, spotless, stainless-steel appliances. Guy had to have every kitchen gadget ever made.

"Have a seat, and I'll get you a beer. Or do you want to fuck first?"

I laughed and sat down at his table. "Let's start with the beer. How are you?"

"Moi?" He waved his hand. "I'm good. Just finished a cat portrait for a crazy woman who changed her mind five thousand times. But you know me, I can go any way anybody wants"—he winked at me—"so it was fine. Made more money off the changes too.

"Oh! And one of my paintings has been accepted into a show in LA. It's a competition really. Doing well could open new doors for me. Can you believe it?"

He put an opened beer bottle in front of me, and I took a big swig before saying anything. He grabbed some fancy bottle of water and a bag of gourmet chips and sat down with me.

"That sounds great. So, is it a nude man or a cat?"

"Both! That's what they like about it. Isn't that fabulous?"

He was as excited as a little kid. He still looked like one some days. Half Korean and half Japanese, Guy was lean but well-muscled, with wide, almond-shaped eyes and straight black hair always streaked with another color. Today, it was yellow, which worked since his last name was Gustavsson. He'd been adopted by two college professors working in Asia. His dad was an engineer. His mom was an artist too.

"That's great. When's the show?"

"November. I'm going to LA for it. Want to come along? We could have a great time. Check out the gay scene."

"You know I don't leave the valley much. But you can tell me about it when you get back."

"Aw, Josh, I would so love to have my own personal cowboy muscleman in the big city." He batted his sleepy, dark brown eyes.

"You know you will do just fine. You always do."

"You are so right." He grabbed a few chips and pushed the bag toward me. "So what's new with you?"

He listened intently as I told him a bit about Hurricane, asking an occasional question. When I finished, he jumped up and made for one of the cabinets.

"I almost forgot. I've got this new hot pepper dip you are just going to love with these chips. I found it in Denver last month."

He grabbed a jar, popped it open, and leaned in close to put it on the table. Then he grabbed a chip, scooped it through the dip, and fed it to me.

"What do you think?"

Whoa, but the pepper was hot. I inhaled another swig of my beer. Guy's hands were on my shoulders now, and I leaned back into his chest. So many of my college nights with him had started this way.

"I like it a lot," I said, turning so I could look in his eyes. "You knew I would. Thanks for getting it for me."

I leaned closer and let him kiss me. Like always, he tasted minty. He moved his hand down my chest to my belt buckle. I was already hard, and he dropped his hand lower and gave me a squeeze.

"Aha," he whispered, "you've been needing to see me. It gets lonely on the range."

I wasn't going to tell him otherwise, but yeah, I was needing him. It was like the night, and especially the morning, with Dane had opened up a big, aching want.

"You know it."

His eyes twinkled. "Let's go in the bedroom. I've redecorated."

I stood up and pulled him close. Like always, he smelled exotic. Sandalwood, he said. The height differential that wasn't a problem in bed forced me to bend over so I could feather kisses along his jaw. I traced the path with my fingers, then grabbed his chin and pushed my tongue past his lips.

Guy groaned dramatically, leaned into me, and wrapped his arms around my waist. As I explored his mouth, he ran his hands down my pants to squeeze my rear.

"In the bedroom," I growled. He scampered down the hall, turning now and again to make sure I was after him. It was a game we played, and today the familiarity was comforting. I knew my part, and I knew how everything would go afterward too.

Guy opened the bedroom door with a flourish and pulled me in.

"What do you think?" He thrust his hands in his pockets, waiting for my answer.

The room was elegant. That had to be the word for it. It was like something you'd see in a really expensive hotel—not that I'd been in one, but I'd seen movies. The walls were a smooth red, like they were covered in fabric. Maybe they were. The big four-poster bed was covered by a black bedspread and a pile of red pillows. Black-and-red-striped drapes that lay across the wooden floor were tied back with thick gold cords that ended in fluffy tassels.

Beyond the bed, Guy had created a sitting area with black leather chairs and low glass tables. The walls were covered with his artwork, a half-dozen large canvases, all male nudes.

"Guy, this is really incredible. It's rich."

He giggled excitedly. "You are the first man to see it."

I looked all around again, and then at him. He was so happy that I liked it. From the day we met, he was always most delighted if I was pleased, didn't matter with what. I never could figure out why my opinion about anything mattered to someone as talented as he was.

I held out my arms and he moved into them. I hugged him hard, and set my head on top of his in the way he either liked or hated depending on his mood.

"It's beautiful. I'm honored." I ran my hands up and down his back and took a step back. "Now, how about you undecorate that lovely body?"

He giggled again as he slipped off his loafers and toed off his socks. Lowering his head so he could look at me through thick eyelashes, he played with his belt buckle. Then he turned around so I could watch the belt snake slowly through each loop.

"Very sexy." I threw myself on the bed and settled down to watch.

He turned around, looked me up and down with wide eyes, and slowly began to pull the shirt out of his black pants.

"Look at those abs! Somebody's been working out hard. I like it."

He grinned and pulled his shirt over his head, squirming his hips left and right. He did love to squirm.

"Pants."

He unzipped and let them fall to his ankles. All I saw were bare balls and his stand-up cock.

"No boxers? I am shocked. Shocked."

Guy giggled.

I rolled to sit at the edge of the bed. "Come here and let me have a closer look."

I swept him into an embrace, nipping and kissing along his collarbone. He settled his hands on my shirt and began to work the buttons. I let him push it off while I nibbled on his nipples, and he shook with held-in laughter. He was a ticklish boy.

I ran my hands up and down his muscled abdomen, groaning my appreciation. I was rock hard.

"Do you need help with your boots, Josh?"

"You know I do."

He turned his back to me, and I stuck out my right leg. He straddled it, bent over, and tugged weakly.

"I like the view."

He giggled again, and I put my left foot on his butt and pushed. My boot popped off, and he tossed it aside.

"Hey, careful! Those are my good boots."

He rolled his eyes, waved his hand, and got in position to remove my other boot.

"Maybe you should stay like that for a while. You look so cute."

"You've got to be kidding. I can't wait that long."

I laughed now. "You can't wait? Heck, I'm the one who never gets any."

"Let me make it all better." He shucked the boot, tossed it aside, and hopped up on the bed next to me, landing on his back. I rolled over on my side beside him and began to run my fingers up and down his belly. He pushed my hand lower, but I batted him away.

"Fine," he said in a pretend huff. He scrambled up to kneel alongside my belly, and I lay back. "I'll just lick your cock then."

His dark eyes glowed as he undid my belt and pants and pulled out my prick. His pointed tongue darted out and slid up the side.

"Oh, yes. More."

Guy had a wicked tongue. Like a snake, he slithered it around my crown in circles till I couldn't take anymore.

"Suck me."

Like he was just waiting for my moan, he opened his mouth and swallowed me deep, running his tongue up and down my length, making sure to hit that special spot just under the head. I thrust up and back and lost myself in the feel and his exaggerated slurpy sounds.

"You know I like that." After a while, I eased him off and sat up. "I think it's time you got some attention. Would you like that?"

His eyes widened. I stroked his jaw, then got up, shed my jeans, and went to the nightstand where I knew he kept condoms and lube.

I rolled him onto his back, grabbed his legs, and pulled him close to the edge of the bed.

He pulled his legs up, and I painted lube down his crack and pushed back on his thighs. He let them fall open wide. Gently, I slipped one finger in and out of his hole, probing deeper with each push until I hit his sweet spot. His ass flew off the bed, then settled back down to rock steady on my finger. I slid in another. He squirmed in earnest.

"Please, Josh. Please, fuck me."

I sheathed my dick and pushed in with a slow, controlled movement.

"Hard," he cried. "Hard, Josh."

But I pulled out and eased in slowly, teasing him.

"You are so pretty like this." Brushing my fingertips up his chest, I pinched his nipples, making him scrunch up his face. "So pretty."

I pushed in hard and watched his eyes fly open. He was hot and tight, his muscles gripping my dick. I grabbed his and pumped it and his ass hard and fast, my sweat dripping on his abs. I could smell his desire.

He inhaled huge, his whole body tightening. Then he yelled and came all over my hand and chest. That sent me over. I shot hard, shuddered, and fell into his arms.

"I've missed you," he sighed. He gazed at me with the look he always gave me. Total acceptance. I could do and be anything with

Guy, and it was okay. Every time I came here, he was happy to see me, and it would be like this forever.

I smeared his cum across his chest with my fingers. He giggled and stuck out his tongue. I put my fingers to his mouth, and he licked them, all the while looking at my face. I smiled and pulled out slowly.

"You stay here. I'll be right back." I headed for the bathroom. It was still done in a dazzling gold and white that I was sure would blind me if I ever came in with a drunk on.

I cleaned up and returned to the bedroom with a warm washcloth and a towel. Guy hadn't moved. Gently, I wiped off his chest, stomach, and ass. I crawled onto the bed and wrapped myself around him, his back to my chest, resting my chin on his shoulder. He rubbed my arms in slow, lazy strokes.

"You want to go have drinks and dinner at Ted's before you drive back?"

Guy knew I loved the steaks at Ted Turner's Montana Grill. "That sounds real good."

We took a shower together, playfully bathing each other. He toweled me off, then helped me put on my clothes and brought me my boots. I watched him pull four different shirts from his closet before he settled on one. It was my favorite, a shiny deep purple shirt with long sleeves. He paired it with tight black jeans. I knew he'd wear a black leather jacket with it.

We walked the few blocks to the Baxter Hotel. It was early yet, and we were seated right away.

Guy ordered a beer and a rare steak with a baked potato for me, then a martini and salmon and a salad for himself. We always got the same thing.

As we waited for our food, he told me all about his latest paintings and some new people he'd met in Bozeman and LA. I had always envied the way he was accepted by everyone.

When our food came, he ordered another martini, and I switched to coffee.

"So, besides the great new horse, how's the ranch?"

"Good. Could be a real good year if we get normal rain." I told him how Sarah was doing, about how full the cabins were, and about the cattle Jesse was running. I skipped any mention of Dane or the downed fence line.

"Why do you ask me about all this stuff anyway? You're not really interested."

"I am too," he said. "It's your way of life, and I'm interested in you."

I felt that uncomfortable guilty tug of my conscience. If I said the word, Guy and I would be in a deep relationship. But as much as I loved him, I wasn't in love. He accepted that.

"Well, I better be getting back."

We paid and headed out through the cavernous two-story lobby to Main Street. Who'd we bump into coming in? Jesse and Dane, on their way into Ted's. Crap.

"Hey, little brother, I wish I'd known you were here. We could have all eaten together," Jesse said. "Guy, how you been?"

The two shook hands while my brain searched for a way to react. Finally, I went with basic introductions.

"Guy, this is Jesse's old Army buddy, Dane. Dane, this is Guy. We hung out together in college."

Guy openly sized up Dane as they shook hands. Dane said something like "good to meet you." I kept my eyes on Guy. The minute lasted forever.

"Have a good dinner," Guy said, and somehow we were finally out on the street.

"Boy, that Army friend is *hot*." Guy was giddy.

"You think?" I kept us moving down the street toward Guy's gallery.

"You don't? Man, I thought muscles were your thing. Is he gay?"

"Don't know."

"You should find out, Josh. He was really eyeing you."

"You got to be kidding."

We walked on to where my truck was parked, and I got in. Standing so his back and the door blocked anyone's view, Guy ran his hands up and down my chest and squeezed my crotch.

"Thanks for visiting, Josh. Come back soon."

"Good luck in LA. Call and tell me how it goes."

"I will."

He watched me back out, and when I glanced in the rearview mirror, he waved. I raised my hand and headed for home.

SEVEN

AFTER that, days passed without my talking to Dane. It seemed to be the way he was going to be. I saw him, walking somewhere around the ranch, or running. He was big into exercise. But he didn't walk or run by me.

I saw Jesse, though, and he told me he and Dane were having a great time together, like old times, and he thought Dane might be beginning to relax. Great, I told him.

To get my mind off Dane, I began to help my aunt make breakfast for the guests. Meant I had to turn in earlier each night, and that helped some.

If Aunt Kate thought it was unusual, she didn't let on. She greeted me with a peck on the cheek and a "How's my favorite nephew today?"

"Your favorite until Jesse shows up," I answered. It was our standard greeting.

She chuckled and pointed me toward the bacon and the grilling stove.

"How's that horse coming, honey?" Since my parents had died, Aunt Kate had tried to be like a mom to me. I didn't appreciate it early on, but I was grateful now.

"I've got a saddle on him, and I've ridden him some." I put the bacon on the griddle, each piece making a spitting hiss as it hit the heat.

She put down the spoon she was scrambling eggs with and turned toward me. Her hazel eyes, now a vivid contrast to the silver hair that had once been gold, sparkled with pride.

"That's wonderful, Josh. When you brought that horse home and I saw him banging up the sides of the trailer, I wondered if even you could do it. But you have a way with horses like I've never seen."

She poured the eggs into a big pan and started scrambling.

"I guess that's what's been keeping you quiet and so off to yourself lately," she added.

I glanced her way, but she didn't look up from the pan, and I was grateful. "Yeah, I don't want the progress to stop." It was partly true.

She was quiet a minute. "Jesse and Dane will be making room for you soon, Josh. Just give them time."

"Oh, I know, Aunt Kate. Dane is Jesse's best friend and all. And they haven't seen each other in a real long time."

"And poor Dane has some things to work through, just like Jesse when he got home. Would you get the dishes out? I'll watch the bacon."

I stepped into the dining room to lay out plates, cups, and silverware, and heat up the food bar pans. When I returned, Aunt Kate handed me the pot of oatmeal. Next came the first big pan of eggs and the pancakes.

"I think you can lay down some more bacon and start the second pan of eggs," she said. "You know, I think Dane might be even more troubled than Jesse was."

"Makes sense, I guess. Dane's been in a lot longer."

"Twelve years," she sighed, wiping her hands on her apron. "Much of it in Afghanistan, from what he says. I think he must have nightmares."

"So, you've been talking to him?"

"Some," she said. "He doesn't talk much. But he is always polite and helpful. And a good listener. He's going to rebuild the laundry room for me—just the way I want."

"No kidding?"

"As soon as he finishes with the door on the calving barn. I think Dane's a good man," she continued. "He just needs some time to get used to the civilized world again, and to try to put some of that fighting behind him." Her voice trailed off as she stacked some more of her golden pancakes on a serving plate.

"You get that bacon and eggs into serving pans, and I think I'm all set," she continued. "When you come back this afternoon, pick up some pork chops for Jesse and Dane for dinner."

AROUND four, I got the pork chops and dropped them at Jesse's, then headed to my barn to clean it. I cranked the radio loud and went to work.

Kenny Chesney was singing about a beach as I moved straw bales. Without warning, a big hand face-planted me into one. Then the hand seized my neck, gripping and flexing in a familiar rhythm that thankfully killed the panic rising in my gut.

"You seem to like rough stuff," I grunted, not bothering to try to get up. The smell of cow barn and sawdust hit my nose as Dane leaned over me, still not letting go of my neck.

"Less than twenty-four hours after being with me, you're fucking someone else? That how you work?" he ground out. He smashed his groin against my ass for emphasis.

"And how do you work, Dane? You're the one who said once was enough. What's this about?"

"I said I was sorry."

"What does that mean exactly?" I was totally bewildered by my current position and his communication.

In response, he jerked me up and wrapped his arm around my waist so my back was flush against his chest. He nuzzled his nose in my neck, scratching me with his rough whiskers, then licked and blew cool air across my skin. I groaned when he slid his hand to my zipper, and my cock jumped. So much for me playing hard to get.

"Fuck, cowboy. I can't get you out of my mind. How about you take down your jeans right now?"

"You're going to do me over a straw bale?"

"You haven't had it that way before? What kind of cowboy are you?"

I shook my head.

"I said take down your jeans. Now."

"You're serious?"

"Fuck, yes. I expect people to do what I say. But I'll help you this once."

He dropped his hands to my belt and undid it. Then he did the same with my pants, pulling them down past my knees. He threw a horse blanket down on the hay bale and pushed me over it again.

"I don't want you to scratch anything important."

I heard the rip of the condom packet. Next thing I felt was a sharp burn as he pushed into me.

I gritted my teeth. "You're hurting me."

"Reprimanding might be a better word." He bent over me and licked my ear. "I don't share, cowboy. At all. Tell me you understand that."

He pushed hard into me again. Silver sparks danced on the edges of my vision, and I tried to crawl away from the hurt. But he grabbed my hips and pulled me back onto him.

"I said, tell me you understand. Tell me you won't be fucking anybody else while you're with me."

"You are nuts. I'm not with—"

A crack rang through the barn. He had slapped my ass.

"Ouch! Stop it."

But he didn't. He hit me again. "Tell me you understand. You won't be fucking anybody else."

"Okay," I gasped, but not fast enough. Another blow landed on my ass. "Dane, I understand, okay?"

"I won't be fucking anybody else. Say it." He smoothed a hand down my back, like he was coaxing me to follow his instructions.

"I understand. I won't be fucking anybody else. Dane, stop it, please."

He stilled and kissed the back of my neck softly. "Good boy, Josh."

He slid his hands down my ass, gentling the sting. He pulled back slow, then readjusted his angle and pushed into me again, hitting my gland. The silver sparks disappeared, replaced by jolts of pleasure and the sweet sensation of being filled with him. He teased my neck with nibbles, bites, and licks. I wanted to say something, but all I managed was a moan.

"Did your artist do you like this? Did he make you feel this good?"

"I did Guy."

He stilled at that, like he hadn't considered the possibility of me topping. What kind of pansy did he think I was?

Before I could come up with a sharp response to set him straight, his hands were on the hay bale alongside my head, trapping me as he thrust fast and hard and deep. I thought he might split me in half.

Then I quit thinking about anything except feeling him inside me. "More."

He bit my shoulder, grabbed my hips, and shoved harder, his thighs banging into mine and knocking me forward. If not for his hands holding me, we'd have toppled over the bale.

"Gonna come, cowboy," he grunted. "Gonna come deep in your ass." I felt the force of his orgasm even as my own sent a fountain of cum across the blanket. I kind of floated away after that.

When I was aware again, Dane was murmuring into my neck. "Whoa, nice. I never fucked someone unconscious before."

He smoothed his hands down my arms and kissed my cheek. Then he pulled me up and grabbed my cock. "You want more?"

Before I could answer, we heard a truck pulling up. I jerked up fast, bumping my head into his chin. "Jesse!"

"Calm down," Dane said like he had nothing to worry about. "I'll go meet him. You clean yourself up."

He slid out of me, pushed my shirt down my back, and tugged my jeans up. I lay unmoving on the bale, totally limp.

"Cowboy," he said gently. "You gotta get moving now." He wrapped his arms around me, pulled me to my feet, and held me. The minute I was steady, he was gone.

When I turned around, he was already zipped up and at the door. He smiled as he watched me fumble with my zipper. Then he stepped out into the sunshine.

I righted my clothes and stashed the blanket and condom among the bales, then sat down to catch my breath. Outside, I heard him greet Jesse cool as could be. Then the door banged as the two of them went into Jesse's house. I made myself go back to cleaning the barn.

JESSE came in about an hour later.

"So you're making dinner for us."

"No. I left pork chops in your fridge. You can make pork chops."

"Please, little brother. You know I'm a bad cook. And you wouldn't want Dane to suffer, would you? Besides," he added. "I want to talk to you about something."

"Talk away."

"It's about Sarah."

A feeling like fear gripped me, and I squeezed hard on the shovel I held.

"Yeah."

"I know you're best friends. You have been forever," he said slowly. "But you don't seem to be dating."

Jesse was quiet for a long time, looking intently at me. The silence grew uncomfortable. I couldn't figure how to end it.

"Are you?" he finally asked. The edge in his voice could have cut hay.

"Am I what?"

"Jeez, Josh, you could make this easier." He was getting angry, but he tried to tamp it down. "For the longest time, I thought you and Sarah were together. Everyone does. But then I started really paying attention, and I don't think you are." His tone was confrontational now. "Are you and Sarah dating?"

Crap. I had never figured on having this conversation with Jesse. In my worst nightmares, I'd never imagined him wanting to date her. If he and Sarah started dating, would he ask her what he had never asked me about my not dating anyone? And if she fell for him, would she feel like she had to tell him the truth I couldn't? And what would happen if they had a conversation like that now, with Dane in the picture? I didn't want to go there.

"Ask Sarah."

"You bastard. I will." He stomped out of the barn.

I let him and Dane make their own dinner.

EIGHT

THE following Saturday was one of those beautiful summer days only Montana can put together. The wind rippled the alfalfa into green waves and pushed the cloud shadows through the valley so fast you'd have thought they belonged to a running giant. But the sun warmed the skin and everything else it touched.

I had loaded up the last of the guests' luggage when Jesse came toward me, moving fast and grinning big like he'd never gotten mad at me about Sarah. He had a plan.

"We're going to the fair in Billings."

"Who's we?"

"You, me, Dane, and Sarah. Now go ask her. We'll meet at the big house in an hour." Then he was gone.

Great. Not only was my brother going to date my best friend, he was going to have me arrange it. I should have said no, but the idea of spending the day with Dane, even with Jesse along, was too appealing.

Sarah was in the kitchen helping Aunt Kate clean up.

"Good morning, beautiful ladies."

"It will be when these dishes are done. Grab a towel and start drying." But Sarah didn't wait for me to grab anything. She threw a towel at me.

"How's my favorite nephew?" Aunt Kate put her hands on her narrow hips, waiting for me to come over and kiss her.

"Fine, until Jesse comes around." I kissed her cheek and caught a whiff of vanilla. She always smelled like vanilla.

"I saved you a cinnamon roll, Josh." She pointed toward the butcher block table where a red and white checkered dish towel hid pure deliciousness.

I helped myself to some milk and took a big bite out of the roll. I could make them myself, but they never tasted as good as hers.

"Mmmm. Still the best, Aunt Kate." I took another bite, savoring the thick, creamy icing.

"Hey, Sarah, speaking of Jesse...."

"I didn't know we were speaking of him."

"Yeah, well, he and Dane and I are going to the fair in Billings. Want to come along?"

"Are you asking, Josh?"

Oh, crap. What to say? I had to let her know what to expect.

"Jesse thought you might like to come along. I'll tour the arts and crafts with you. Promise."

She smiled bright. She liked those. "When are we leaving?"

"In an hour."

"Well then, Sarah, you'd better go get ready," Aunt Kate said. "I'll finish up here." She waved us both out of the kitchen.

An hour later, Sarah and I climbed into the backseat and Dane and Jesse into the front of my brother's truck. As he drove, Jesse kept up a conversation with Dane about the cattle he wanted to see and watching the afternoon motorcycle stunt show.

Every now and then, I'd catch him looking at Sarah and me in the backseat. At her, really. But he'd glance at me too, like he was checking out where my hands were and how far apart we were sitting. I couldn't quite convince myself that I was imagining it.

When we arrived, Jesse and Dane took off right away for the stunt show.

"Meet you at the Ferris wheel in three hours," Jesse called.

Sarah steered me straight for the arts and crafts. She'd taken up knitting a few years ago and liked to see what others were making. She spent a lot of time fingering the sweaters, shawls, hats, and scarves, exclaiming about the feel of the yarn and the color combinations. I didn't get it myself, but I touched what she pointed out and said I liked the colors when she asked.

I liked the fine arts exhibit better, especially the horse paintings, and we agreed on our favorites. We stopped to eat before heading over to the midway to meet up with Jesse and Dane.

"So anything happening between you and Dane?" she asked before biting into a sugary elephant ear.

I'd just gobbled down a mustard-drenched corn dog myself, and it took me a minute to get past the tangy taste and answer. "He's spending most of his time with Jesse."

"I suppose they have a lot of catching up to do."

"Yeah, I think so."

"And how are you and Dane getting along?" She looked at me sideways.

"You're fishing."

"I am. Is he gay?"

For a minute, I debated telling her the truth. I'd always told her the truth. And she'd kept my secret.

"Yeah, he is. Jesse doesn't know."

"And?"

"I think he's got some post-traumatic stress issues."

"I wouldn't be surprised. Aunt Kate says he's seen a lot of fighting for a long time, and Jesse says Dane has admitted he's got some stuff to deal with."

"You're talking that much with Jesse now?" Crap, I shouldn't have said that, especially not that way. My stomach cramped, and not because of the corn dog.

She gave me a funny look. "I always talk to your brother. I see him at least once a day, you know."

She didn't understand yet that Jesse had set his sights on her. But before I could decide whether to tell her and ask her not to go out with him, she was on me again.

"I asked about Dane because I'm worried about you. Should I be?"

We were walking through the midway games. The crowd was sparse but would pick up once night and the midway's mass of multicolored lights came on. Right now though, every one of the rough-looking, tattooed carnies called out to me to try to win my girl a stuffed something by shooting guns or baskets.

When I didn't answer her question right away, Sarah followed up. "What's happening with the two of you?"

What a good question. Darned if I knew. Should I tell her I'd had the best sex ever, then been punched out the next morning? That I couldn't get the guy off my mind? That I'd never been with anybody who controlled sex like he did, and it was so hot I couldn't imagine enjoying it as much with anyone else again?

"Nothing's happening really. He runs real hot and cold."

"What do you mean?"

"He'll be friendly one day, then not talk to me for a couple days even though we see each other. It's a common PTSD thing. Jesse was that way when he got back too, real wrapped up in whatever he was remembering in his own head. But he got over it."

"He must have," she agreed.

Sarah stopped then to consider one of the game booths, the one where you cast a line to try to land the sinker in one of a couple dozen fish bowls—except that the sinker has no real weight on it so it won't fall true.

"You know, I took a continuing ed class that talked about PTSD. That's not easy stuff to deal with, Josh. Some people don't ever get over it."

"I know."

"So maybe you should just steer clear of getting involved with Dane? You don't need that kind of trouble."

"Yes, mother."

She smiled real sweet. "Try to win me something, will you, Josh?"

"You know this game is rigged."

"Please?"

I shook my head, but I still bought five chances. The carny, a bald guy of indeterminate age and missing a few teeth, was all over me. "Come on, cowboy. Win your pretty girl a nice prize. You can do it. This is kids' play. What's your name, honey?"

"Sarah."

"And what do you want, Sarah?" he asked with a creepy-crawly leer. His question held way too many innuendoes, and his eyes didn't leave Sarah's chest as he pushed a fishing pole in my hand. She ignored him to concentrate on my fishing technique.

"Try that bowl there, Josh. That looks like a good one."

So I tried, five times. No luck. I knew I wouldn't win.

Sarah laughed and slipped her arm through mine. "I know you can do it. Win me a big stuffed bear, won't you, Josh?"

"You are serious about this, aren't you?"

She batted her eyes, and I pulled out my wallet again to buy five more chances.

"Come on, Josh," the carny said like we'd been friends forever. "You can do it. A big strapping cowboy like you. You can't let your little lady down."

A minute and five more tries later, I let my little lady down.

I cast Sarah a questioning look. She laughed, her eyes sparkling with fun, and I had to laugh too. But I'd had it with the creepy carny.

"Hey, little lady, I see Jesse and Dane by the Ferris wheel. Let's go." I put my arm around her waist and pulled her away from the booth.

"Cowboy, you can't quit now," he called after me. "You're going to get lucky. I can feel it."

"Yes, Josh, you're going to get lucky," Sarah teased.

"But not with you. Come on."

We were still arm in arm and laughing when we caught up with my brother and Dane. I swear, both of them cast grim looks my way, but she didn't notice.

Sarah could spot a misbehaving kid behind her back, but she was not seeing what was right in front of her. I wondered what was wrong with her, but I was glad too. If she kept up this way, maybe nothing would come of Jesse's plan for her.

"So how were the cattle and motorcycles?" she asked.

"Thankfully, not on the track together," Dane answered.

"Dane, my man, what an idea. I see a fair show in our future." Jesse's eyes sparkled in fun. He winked at Sarah and poked Dane in the ribs.

"That was a joke, Jess."

"Can't you see it, though? Motorcycles running a tough hill course and dodging cattle too? Or do they win points if they go vertical after hitting the cows? We could make some good money."

"No."

"Just for that," Jesse shot back, "I'm not riding the Ferris wheel with you. Come on, Sarah."

He grabbed her arm, shot her one of his dimpled grins, and led her to the end of the line. She laughed and let him move her along, pausing just long enough to wave in my direction.

"Well wasn't that a smooth maneuver?" Dane asked.

"He's got good moves."

"I like yours a little bit better," he whispered, an evil look in his eyes.

"Just a little bit, huh?"

"Can't make you overconfident."

"No fear of that happening. Now shut up, will you?" I glanced around to see if anyone was looking at us. I needed to adjust my jeans in the worst way.

Dane laughed. "Come on. Let's ride the Ferris wheel."

We ended up two chairs behind Jesse and Sarah. Jesse had draped his arm over the back of the seat, and the two of them began an animated conversation.

"So what do you think about those two?" Dane asked.

"I don't think there is a 'those two'. He's not her type."

Dane turned to look at me. "You really believe that, cowboy?"

"Yeah. Hey, look over there. You can see the Rims."

"What are the Rims?"

"Those two long cliffs. They divide the city. See? The one to the north is about five hundred feet high, and there's the one to the east. And there to the southeast is the Yellowstone River, which goes by our place."

"It all looks peaceful and pretty from up here." Dane sighed. "Even a war zone can look peaceful just before the helo drops you into it."

He was quiet for a bit, and the ride sped up, whirling us up to the sky, then down to the ground and around again. Whenever the ride took us high into the air, I rubbed my thumb across the knuckles of his left hand, which was resting loosely on the grab bar.

"I've always liked how things look from the air," he said, watching me do it. "Guess that's why the Ferris wheel was always my favorite ride."

"I was afraid of them when I was a kid."

"I'll protect you, cowboy."

"Will you now?"

"At least until I hurt you again," he said softly. His face colored. "I'm sorry about punching you that morning."

He was gripping the safety bar hard now, and I laid my hand over his. "It's okay, Dane. Really. I know it's the PTSD."

"Do you?"

"Jesse had it. Talk about it with him."

"Yeah, I am." He paused, like he was debating saying more. Then he changed the subject. "So what midway ride did you like best?"

"I always wanted to ride the ponies."

"Imagine that." Dane was smiling now, and I was glad.

"Yeah, but the guys running the rides never let me go fast."

Dane laughed. "And now you're too big for the ponies."

"Sad but true."

"What ride did Jesse like?"

"He didn't do rides. He spent all his money on games. Especially ones involving rifles."

"So that's how he was the only one who could beat me on the shooting range."

"Yeah. I imagine he'll drag us there next."

He did. He and Sarah were beaming when we met up with them after the ride. She was having a good time. He looked like he thought his plan was going just fine. I felt uneasy.

"Okay, guys, time for some shooting practice," he said gleefully. "One of us will win you something, Sarah."

"I hope so," she said, casting a look my way.

"Hey, I told you that fish bowl thing was fixed."

"Sure it was, little brother," Jesse mocked. "Let's see how you do shooting."

"I am not competing with you. Let Dane give it a try."

I was insistent about not going up against Jesse. I didn't need to prove anything. I wouldn't have proved anything anyway.

Dane was willing to try, and we stopped at a shooting booth with rows of moving ducks for targets. Jesse let Dane go first, and Dane picked up the rifle and hit them all, one after the other without stopping.

The carny, a short, thin man with a cigarette pack wrapped in each sleeve of his dirty white T-shirt, set Dane up again.

"You can't stop now, Ranger," he insisted. He'd spotted Dane's tattoo. Well, really, you couldn't miss it.

Bound in his tight red shirt, Dane's arm muscles were that much more noticeable where the shirt sleeves ended. Each time his arm moved, the tattoo jumped like it was alive. The skull's grin got bigger too. Kind of spooky, really.

A crowd began to form quietly behind us, both men and women stopping to watch. The women were watching Dane. The men had their eyes on the targets, which all fell down again.

"Another go, Ranger? Come on. You can't stop now," the carny urged. A greasy grin creased his dark, gaunt face, and his body vibrated as he pondered the financial possibilities not just of Jesse and Dane, but the crowd too. He'd be able to keep himself in cigarettes for a few days more for sure.

Jesse held out a bill, and the carny snatched it. "That's it, boys. Just pretend those ducks are al-Qaeda."

Something dark flickered across Dane's face at the carny's remark, there and gone in a fraction of a second. Nobody but me noticed.

Dane began shooting again. He wiped out the top row, then missed three targets one after the other on the lower level. He closed his eyes and put the rifle on the counter.

"Hey, you aren't done," the carny cried.

"I'm done."

"But—"

"I'm done."

The carny eyed the crowd in desperation and turned to my brother.

"How about you, cowboy? You gonna show this Ranger how a Montana man shoots?"

Jesse laughed and handed the man another bill. He was aware of the crowd, and of Sarah's eyes watching him.

"You bet. Set them up."

"The gun pulls left," Dane said.

Jesse picked it up and looked down the sights. "Got it."

He fired in rapid succession. Every sitting duck fell down.

"Again," he said, his eyes never leaving the back of the booth. He was totally focused on the game.

As soon as the carny said, "All set," Jesse fired again, one fast shot after the other. All the targets toppled. If the gun could have smoked, it would have.

"Again."

He repeated his performance three more times, then put down the rifle.

"Think I'm about done here, Mister," he said. "What did I win?"

"Don't stop now, cowboy. You're on a roll," the carny urged. "You got a crowd too."

"It's Ranger, same as him." Jesse pointed respectfully at Dane. "And I'm done."

"Come on. Try again?" But the disappointed carny knew enough to give up. He looked at all the stuffed animals hanging over our heads and then at Sarah.

"Which one you want, honey?"

Sarah pointed to the biggest teddy bear in the bunch, and he pulled it down and gave it to her. It had to be the size of a five-year-old.

Jesse's eyes shone bright as her face lit up.

"Are you really giving it to me, Jesse?" she asked. Her arms hugged the fuzzy brown thing to her chest.

"You bet, Sarah."

"It's fabulous," she insisted, moving closer to him.

"Hey, soldier." The carny held a small blue bear out to Dane, who seemed not to comprehend the gesture. "You won one too, man." He waved the bear insistently.

Dane looked around at the folks who were still watching. He pointed to a young girl, about ten, who had stopped with her parents to watch.

"Give it to her," he told the carny.

The girl looked at her father, who nodded at her and then at Dane. She smiled shyly when she took the bear, but Dane was already walking away.

I picked up my pace to catch him. "That was a nice gesture."

He ignored me and turned around to look for Jesse, who was twenty feet behind us with Sarah.

"So what are we doing next?" he asked my brother.

Jesse looked at Sarah. "Anything else you want to see?"

Sarah looked at me. "We still haven't toured the horse barns, Josh."

"We don't need to." I figured Dane might want to head back to the ranch. I knew something was bothering him, and we still had a two-hour drive ahead of us.

But Dane surprised me. "That sounds like fun, cowboy. Which way?"

I glanced at Jesse. "Sure, why not?" he agreed.

So I pointed us toward the Super Barn. I knew it like I knew my own barn. A show was just beginning, and we took some seats in the half-filled stands. Dane sat next to me right away, and I was so pleased I didn't even bother to worry that that left Jesse and Sarah sitting together.

It was a class of year-old geldings, presented by their teenaged handlers.

"What are you watching for?" Dane asked.

"In the horse, does it meet the specifications of its breed? How attractive is its head. Does it have a strong back, a deep chest, overall soundness. Is it nervous, or making smooth transitions or rough."

We watched the mix of American quarter horses, paints, and saddlebreds as their handlers led them around the arena. Some of the kids were nervous, and it transmitted to their horses in a bad way.

"See there? That one just balked. Not good. But that is on the handler or trainer, maybe. Overall, this is a really good group. There's a lot of things that go into showing."

"Did you show horses here when you were young?"

"Yeah."

"How'd you do?"

"Won grand champion a couple times."

"That the top award?"

"Yeah."

Dane snorted. "And you're not bragging about that?"

I looked at him, and he was grinning at me. My face heated up as I tried to explain.

"I never have understood why I'm good with horses. I just always have been, you know? I have had to study it, sure, but a lot of it, it was like I just knew it from the time I knew anything. So what's to brag about?"

Dane bumped my ribs with his elbow. "It's okay, cowboy. I think it's commendable. Cute, even."

"Cute?" I said too loudly.

Immediately, I glanced around. Jesse was totally absorbed in whatever Sarah was saying, and there weren't many people sitting close to us, so I was okay. Still, I whispered my next comments.

"Cute is hardly…."

"Masculine enough?" Dane offered, laughing outright. He leaned in close and whispered, "You just have to accept that you're cute, cowboy."

"Whatever." I turned back to watching the horses.

Dane leaned over once more and whispered again, "But you're masculine enough too. I'd name you first in class."

"Would you stop? I'm already hard."

He laughed for a long time, then left me alone. Not too long after, we headed home.

On the ride back, I was with Sarah again, and her gigantic stuffed bear, in the backseat. I think Dane fell asleep. The only sound in the truck cab was the music from the radio, and the station played way too many songs about country boys and girls getting down on the farm, that's for sure.

NINE

DESPITE all his teasing at the fair, Dane fell back into his pattern of ignoring me for a few days once we got back home.

I thought it was darned nasty too, considering how horny he'd made me. Still, I let him stay standoffish until one morning when I passed the calving barn and heard the table saw going. It was time I made another attempt at pursuing him, I decided, or gave him another chance to push me away.

He was making impressive progress on the barn door. He wasn't fixing it; he was building two new ones, cutting fresh boards and supports. He had a decorative pattern going too that mimicked some of the woodwork in the great hall of the big house. Uncle Karl was going to love it.

I walked inside and sat down on the pile of boards next to where he was running the table saw and waited for him to stop what he was doing.

"This is going to look great when you're done."

"Thanks."

He took off his protective goggles and ogled me.

"That is so not fair," I complained, tilting my head so I looked at him from beneath the brim of my hat. I was trying to be sexy.

"What?" he asked. Like he didn't know.

"You haven't come near me in days, but you keep stripping me naked with your eyes."

"You missing me, cowboy? You sound like a horny girl."

I leaned back and splayed my knees. "Like what you see?"

He made like he was inspecting the wood he'd just cut and ignored me completely.

"You are not fair." I was sporting wood.

All he did was chuckle when he noticed.

"You know, you ought to just let me fuck you." I meant it to be suave, channeling George Clooney, but I sounded more like the dorkiest kid in high school.

"I don't bottom."

"You're kidding."

"Ever."

"Don't you want to experience the other? Have some variety?"

"Nope."

"Don't you want to feel what it's like to have someone so deep inside you, you hope they'll never leave?"

"Cowboy, that's loneliness talking."

"Is not."

"Then it's love bullshit."

"You don't believe in love?" I was beginning not to like this conversation.

"Nope."

"Good to know."

It was all I could think of to say. He hadn't just rejected me, he'd pretty much stamped *idiot* across my forehead. I had to get out of there before I said something really stupid.

I stood up. "Guess I'll go get ready to give some riding lessons."

"Have a good time." He turned on the saw again.

I HAD a trail ride after the riding lessons, then took care of the horses, so it was pretty much the end of the day before I thought seriously about Dane again.

By then, most everybody was in the bunkhouse or the big house eating dinner. I was the only one near any of the barns when I heard shouting in the calving barn. Even above the whining of the saw, I knew it was Dane.

As I got closer, the words became clearer. "Get down! Get down! Marshall, stay put.... He's hit, he's hit. Where are those fucking helos?"

I started running.

When I threw open the door, I smelled blood before anything else. Dane was still yelling, but it was a long, choking "Noooo" now.

He sat cross-legged on the floor, rocking back and forth, his right hand clutching his left. Blood spurted between his fingers. It was pooling in his lap and splattered across the wall behind the whirring saw.

I yelled at him as I dashed for the electric cord to unplug it. I was afraid I'd see fingers around the saw. I didn't want to look, but I did, and thank God there weren't any. I might have heaved.

I yanked out the plug, and the saw whined to a stop. When I grabbed Dane's shoulder, he looked up, but he wasn't seeing me.

"Help Marshall, you dumb fuck."

"Dane! It's Josh. Dane, what happened?"

"What do you think happened?" he shouted. "We were hit. Help Marshall."

He pushed me away with his bloody hands, knocking me to the floor. I shook my head, trying to figure what to do. I was terrified he was going to bleed to death.

"Dane, you're here at the ranch, remember?" I got up and approached him more cautiously. "Come on, Dane, let me help you. You're scaring me."

"Help Marshall!" He shoved at me again.

"Okay. Okay."

I decided to go with his hallucination. "Folks are on their way to help Marshall. I'm here to help you. Let me look at your hands now."

That seemed to do it. He held them up to me. Both of them trembled. Mine did too as I reached to touch his left one. He'd cut it, and badly if all the blood was any indication. I pulled off my belt and reached for his arm, but he batted me away.

"Help Marshall or I'll shoot you," he snarled. "Where's my goddamn gun?"

"Relax, help's coming for him," I repeated, wrestling with his flying arms to try to grab the left one.

When I had it, I tied my belt around his arm above the elbow and pulled tight, then waved the buckle end in front of his face.

"You hold this. You hear me? You hold this while I go check on… things." I pushed the buckle into his good hand. "You just sit here and hold that."

I knew I needed help, and I knew I didn't want a whole bunch of people seeing him like this.

I headed deeper into the barn. It had the equivalent of an operating room for cattle. Uncle Karl could perform most of the routine operations himself. There'd be something to use for a bandage, along with a radio. We kept them scattered across the ranch, and Uncle Karl, Jesse, and Aunt Kate always had one with them. I found it right where it was supposed to be and turned it on. I let out a slow breath and took in another so I wouldn't sound as panicked as I felt when I talked.

"Jesse, this is Josh. Where you at?"

All I heard was static.

"Jesse, this is Josh, over."

"What's up?"

"Where you at, over."

"I'll be at the horse barn in four."

"Make it the calving barn in one. I... I need you."

I hoped I sounded calm. Uncle Karl was always telling us to watch what we said on the radios. Guests might hear.

"Roger," Jesse said.

I found some clean rags and a bottle of antiseptic and headed back to Dane.

He was still rocking and choking out Marshall's name as he stared off into the dark of the far end of the barn.

"Dane," I said loudly. "Jesse's coming. Marshall's going to be okay."

"He's dead," Dane groaned.

I crouched near him and checked to make sure the tourniquet was holding. It was an awfully long minute before I heard Jesse's truck drive up and come to a stop. Dane got quiet and closed his eyes. His head began to droop.

"Dane. Hang on." I grabbed at his good arm. "Hang on. Jesse's here."

"Aw, fuck, Dane," Jesse's words came out above my head.

Dane jerked his head up and opened his eyes.

"Marshall's dead, isn't he?" he said to Jesse.

"He's been yelling 'Get down' and something about a guy named Marshall since I got here. It's like he's somewhere else."

I looked up at my brother with relief and made to hand him the rags and antiseptic, but he put his hand on Dane's shoulder instead.

"Dane, let me take a look at you."

Dane raised his bloody hands again. They shook violently now.

Jesse turned over the left one to reveal a gaping, bloody slice below the pinkie knuckle.

"Call Uncle Karl," he said to me.

"I'm here." The voice came from the doorway. He evaluated the situation in an instant, and turned to me.

"Get Kate on the radio and tell her we're headed to Livingston Memorial. Tell her to bring out a bunch of clean towels as the truck comes by the house. And stay calm. Jesse, pour some of that antiseptic over his hand, then try to hold it together. Watch out, he might swing at you because it's going to hurt. Then let's get him into your truck."

I ran back to the radio and relayed the message. By the time I'd finished talking to Aunt Kate, Uncle Karl was climbing into Jesse's truck on the driver's side. Dane sat in the middle, next to my brother, his head tipped far back on the seat, his eyes closed.

"I'll come too."

"You stay here," Uncle Karl said. "You did a good job, Josh."

Jesse leaned across Dane to talk to me. "He's had a flashback, Josh. I figured he had PTSD, but not like this."

Uncle Karl started the truck, and they took off. I stood in the dust and watched them slow down to grab the towels from Aunt Kate, then speed up. I figured Uncle Karl would keep his foot to the floor all the way to Livingston.

I don't know how long I stared down the road. Then I went back inside the barn to clean up. I choked a couple of times, but I finished the job. I wanted it to look like nothing had happened when Dane got back.

TEN

I HEADED to my house and saddled up Hector. I had been trying for a couple of days to get out and check the fence line by the national forest. Now I was glad to have something to do to pass the time.

Hurricane snorted at me when he saw that he wasn't going to be getting my attention.

"Soon, boy."

Hector was antsy when I swung into the saddle. Maybe he smelled the blood on my clothes. I nudged him into a trot and then a gallop, and he settled in.

Before I was even aware of it, we were at the fence line. He headed straight for the gate. We went through, I closed it, and we trotted through the woods.

My mind raced, replaying the scene in the barn. I was afraid for Dane. I was afraid the accident might make him leave, and I wanted him to stay. No matter that he kept pushing me away, I wanted him to stay.

I was mad that I couldn't go with him. I should be there. I knew I should. Would he wonder why I wasn't? I argued with myself about that for a while before I realized he likely wouldn't remember I'd been part of it. And if he did remember, he might be embarrassed. And that might make him push me away even more.

A vision of Brittany flashed in my mind. She was standing in that meadow, the rain coming down hard, stubbornly refusing to mount up, desperately demanding my attention, and right then I knew the ache and longing she must have felt. What a pathetic mess. Yeah, I'd become a muddle of teenage angst again over a man who was probably already worried I was too young for him. He'd be dumping my butt for good as soon as he got back. If he came back.

When I'd finally stopped thinking about it all, the sun was sinking. I turned Hector toward home. I didn't want to hit a hole in the dark or scare up a snake that might startle him.

Near the fence line again, a sudden shimmer in the grass caught my eye. I swung off Hector to look closely. It was an empty beer can. Three more were scattered nearby, all shiny and new. They hadn't been out here long.

Someone had been back up here. But the fence line was intact. What were they up to? All kinds of nonsense ideas flashed through my mind, all of them drenched in blood. Dane's blood. I was scaring myself.

I put the cans in my saddlebag and headed for home.

Once I'd taken care of Hector and given Hurricane and Sugarpie some feed, I went to my place. I grabbed a beer and sat on Gran's old rocker on my front porch, staring at Jesse's house. Like I thought that would make them all get back sooner. I didn't know what else to do. I was stuck in that horrible worrying time, where you're waiting for news and not getting it, and time seems like it never moves. I'd been there before, a bunch of times, over Jesse.

Somehow though I fell asleep, because the next thing I knew, I was awake and my neck was stiff.

Jesse's truck was parked in front of his place, and the house was dark.

I pulled myself out of the chair and headed toward it. I don't know why exactly. I knew I wasn't going to go inside and wake Jesse and Dane up. Heck, Dane might not even be there. Maybe he'd had to stay at the hospital. I knew all that, but it was like I believed standing in front of the house might give me some clues to what had happened.

So that's what I did. I stared at the bedroom window I knew was Dane's.

"Hey, cowboy."

The voice was low, but I jumped like it was a shout. I glanced around wildly until I saw him. It took me a minute. He was lying flat on his back on the porch floor.

"What are you doing?"

"I can't sleep."

"Didn't they give you anything for that?"

"They wanted to. I don't like to take stuff." He raised his head slightly and looked at me. "Why don't you come up here so I don't have to move."

"Sure." I sat down next to him, looking at his face. His left hand, resting on his stomach, was wrapped up so it looked three times normal size.

"Are you okay?"

"I will be. It looked worse than it was. I was lucky. Missed the bone."

He looked at me like he was worried and put his good hand on my knee. It felt good. "I didn't scare you too bad, did I?"

His question surprised me and made me uncomfortable. Why was he making this about me?

"How many stitches did it take?"

"A bunch. But this big bandage can come off in a couple of days. I'm going to be fine. Did I scare you?"

"What do you mean? You had an accident. Stuff like that happens on ranches. You deal with what you find."

"And you did a good job dealing." Dane sighed. "Josh, look at me."

I made myself do it.

"I would have been scared if I'd run in that barn, seen you all bloody, and heard you talking nonsense."

"It wasn't nonsense."

"I've got PTSD."

"I know. Post traumatic stress disorder, from the wars. Lots of guys have it. Jesse had it."

"I've got a pretty bad case."

"I can deal with it."

"You think?"

"I don't have to have been there to be able to have some sympathy, you know. And you can go talk to people about it and take drugs."

Almost before I'd finished, he spoke in a steely sharp voice. "I don't want to talk to people or take drugs."

"I'm sorry. Don't get upset, okay? Wrong thing to say. I won't say it again."

He had turned his head away from me. I knew he was angry, and I didn't know what to do. I wanted to jump up and run back to my house, but the hand still gripping my knee was holding me down. I put my hand on his. His was cold.

"Come on, let's get you inside. You're going to freeze."

He looked up at the ceiling and closed his eyes.

"I killed a lot of people."

I didn't answer right away, searching for the right thing to say. "I think that's the point."

He grimaced. "Some of them were women and children."

"That happens." I wanted to reassure him, to make him understand I was okay with whatever he'd done.

"I might have been able to do something different."

"You can't change the past."

His eyes flew open.

"Fuck you, cowboy." Dane's chest heaved with breaths that came fast and loud, and he shook my hand off his like he didn't want anything to do with me. "You think that up all by yourself? Maybe you should go into counseling."

I knew something about counseling. The day my parents died, I'd been mad at my mom. When I learned about the accident, I stopped talking. I didn't talk for weeks. Aunt Kate was so worried she took me to a counselor. I didn't talk there either, and she finally stopped taking me. But I'd listened some, and I did start talking again later on my own. And I made it a point to never get mad at anybody again.

Without thinking, I put my hand on Dane's chest and began to rub it in circles like my mom used to, slowly expanding the area until I'd touched everything from his collarbone to his belt buckle. His breathing slowed down.

"It was a stupid thing to say. I do that a lot around you. I'm sorry."

He clenched his eyes shut and covered his face with his good arm. He shuddered, drawing in hard breaths. "It's not you, cowboy. It's… not you."

I rubbed his chest again for a few minutes. "Let's go inside now, okay? You're cold."

He let me help him into the living room, and he lay down on the couch. I grabbed the afghan draped across the back and covered him up, tucking it in around his shoulders, sides, and feet.

"Thanks, mom."

"I don't want to be your mom."

"What do you want?"

"You know." I stared hard and long into his eyes, till he shut them.

I sat down on the coffee table and watched him till he fell asleep. Then I slipped out the door and went back to my house.

ELEVEN

DANE was in Jesse's kitchen trying to make coffee one-handed when I walked in. He'd already spilled water on the counter and was having trouble with the coffee can.

"How about I make us breakfast?" I tried real hard to make sure it didn't sound like I thought he was crippled or incapable.

"I can do it." He concentrated harder on working the can opener.

"I know you can, but I'm a better cook." I put on my most charming smile.

He was scowling when he looked up, but the smile must have been right.

"That's a good idea, cowboy. I'll just sit down and wait."

"You can set the table. What you want?"

"An omelet?"

"Coming up."

He sat down and I went to work. Got the coffee going and started chopping onions, peppers, and cheese. Gave him a cup of coffee and put the bacon and the timer on.

The silence was comfortable. I'd just poured the chopped ingredients onto the eggs when I felt him behind me.

"Smells good," Dane whispered. His breath tickled my neck.

"Me or the bacon?"

He swatted my ass with his good hand. "Wiseass."

"Sore ass now."

"Poor baby." He began to rub my butt. My cock hardened. "Better?"

I groaned. He rested his bandaged hand on my hip and slid his good one around to palm me.

"Much better now, aren't you, cowboy?"

Oh yeah. I turned my face toward his and bumped into his lips. Like that, his tongue was in my mouth exploring. He tasted so good. I wanted to turn into him, but he held me in place. He finished the kiss with a light brush of his lips across mine.

"Don't want you to burn my breakfast. I'll just sit down now and wait."

I kept my back to him, trying to tamp down my desire and frustration as I folded the omelet.

"You're just a tease, is that it?"

He chuckled. "That wasn't a tease, it was a taste."

My heart sped up, and my brain froze. Images from my daydreams—Dane fucking me, me sucking him half-crazy, sweat and cum and groans—flashed through my mind. And the timer went off.

The omelets and the bacon were done. Hard or not, I had to turn around and serve them. My face was hot. I didn't look up as I crossed to the table and slid his onto his plate.

He rubbed my ass again. "You look real cute, cowboy."

"Cute. Jeez."

He ignored me and dug into his omelet.

"Without a doubt, this is one of the best I've ever had," he said between bites.

"Ass or omelet?"

He laughed outright then, and shot me a come-on look.

"We'll just have to see about the first, won't we?"

"Talk, talk." I slid into my seat and started to eat.

"Cowboy, you are going to be one sorry ass when this bandage comes off my hand."

"Promises, promises."

I pushed a piece of bacon in my mouth. When I chanced a look at him, he was staring at me, a look full of want. He pointed his fork at me.

"Promise," he said.

I knew the grin on my face looked ridiculous, but I didn't care. I'd just won something important, even if I wasn't sure what. "So how is your hand feeling?"

"Is that you being eager or trying to change the subject?"

I smiled, took a bite of omelet, and made a motion about my mouth being full. He grinned and shook his head.

"It doesn't hurt too bad right now." Then he changed the subject. "So what are you doing today?"

"Trail ride, then a trip to the feed store in Livingston. Did Jesse say what he was up to?"

"Going to go check that fence line again, then head out to some auction. I might go along."

"Crap. With everything last night, I forgot. I found beer cans by the fence line."

Dane was instantly totally serious. "How many?"

"Four."

"No telling how many guys that might mean. I'll call him right now." He disappeared up the stairs to his room.

I KNEW I was cursed the minute I heard the voice behind me outside the feed store.

"So, Brooks, how you doing with that mustang?" Ray Hanson sneered.

I concentrated on loading the feed I'd just bought into my truck.

"Good, Ray. Things are good." I didn't turn around, hoping he'd move on. He didn't.

"Then I'll stop by tomorrow afternoon and see."

"Sorry, Ray, I don't have time. Trail rides and all, you know."

"No bother. I'll just look him over. Be there around five."

He was moving toward his truck when I turned around to protest.

"Ray. Can't do it."

"Five," he yelled. He climbed into his truck and took off, his tires spitting gravel.

All the way home, I worried about what to do. I could already hear what Jesse would say, and I didn't want to, especially in front of Dane. Maybe Hanson was just playing with me. Yeah, that was it.

WHEN Hanson didn't show up at five or six the next day, I decided I'd been right. I turned Hurricane out into the corral and got my saddle out. He tossed his head when I put it on the ground next to him. He was definitely ready to go.

I rubbed his neck and forehead. "Today we'll take that long ride I promised."

I didn't even turn around right away when the truck pulled up. I figured it was Jesse or Dane.

"What you doing there, Brooks?" a voice called out.

It was Hanson's foreman, Mel Evans, with Hanson right beside him, walking toward the corral. My gut dropped into my boots.

"You got a saddle on that gelding." It wasn't so much a question as a statement from Hanson.

The two of them had reached the fence across the corral from Hurricane and me. Hanson looked angry. Evans looked like he was ready to fight. He always looked that way. Rumor was, he'd served time in prison.

"Nope." I hoped my lie was convincing. I was never much good at it.

"But you got far enough to try?" Hanson asked, draping his arms on the top of the fence. He didn't look happy.

"Nope. Not making much progress at all, Ray. Sorry you wasted the trip."

As I walked through the corral toward them, Hurricane moved back closer to the barn. He remembered Hanson.

"You're lying, Brooks," Evans said.

"Nope." I climbed the fence and dropped down within five feet of him, hoping it was a scary enough maneuver.

"Boys, let's be peaceable. And Melvin," Hanson said slowly, "shut up." Evans grimaced and Hanson gave me a nod. But something in his eyes said he wasn't really interested in being peaceable.

"So, Brooks, show me what he can do." It wasn't a request.

"You're seeing it, Ray. He stands on the far side of the corral when I try to do anything."

"Put him through his paces, Josh."

"No paces to show, Ray."

Clearly Hanson didn't believe me. He whistled and darned if Hurricane didn't choose that moment to trot round the corral, still making sure to stay clear of Hanson. Showoff.

"I'd say you are making progress, Brooks."

"And you were lying," Evans snapped.

Hanson cut him off. "What else can the horse do?"

The butterflies in my stomach morphed into 747s. "That's it."

"How'd you do it?" Hanson asked. Both men took a step toward me.

"Josh, where the hell you been?"

I turned to see Jesse striding my way. He didn't look happy.

"Aunt Kate needs you in the kitchen," he said. It sounded like an order.

"Hey," I said, but Jesse ignored me.

"What brings you out here, Ray?" my brother asked.

He had stopped close enough that we all made a triangle now, me the point on top and Jesse facing off against Hanson and Evans across the bottom.

"Came out to see how Josh was doing with that horse he bought from me. You know, just two horse trainers comparing methods," Hanson replied. His tone was conversational but not friendly.

"Not much to show," Jesse said. "Right, Josh?"

"Right."

"And like I said," Jesse continued, "Aunt Kate needs Josh's help in the kitchen." He looked Hanson in the eye. "Sorry you came out here for nothing, Ray."

"Wasn't for nothing," Hanson said. "Thanks for the show, Josh. We'll be taking off."

"Yeah," Evans said, "so you can go be kitchen help." He sneered the last two words, and he and Hanson headed for their truck.

Jesse didn't say a word until the truck was down the driveway.

"Didn't I tell you to stay away from him? What were you thinking having them out here?"

"I didn't 'have' them here. Hanson invited himself when he saw me at the feed store yesterday. And thanks for making me sound like wimpy kitchen help. Jeez, Jesse."

"Forget that. What did Hanson see?"

I grimaced. I didn't want to, but I had to tell him. "Hurricane responded when he whistled. And he saw the saddle, of course."

"Oh, fuck. Don't you think we have enough problems with the fence line? Now you gotta ramp up this competition between you and Hanson?"

"It wasn't me, Jesse, it was him."

Jesse took off his hat, combed his fingers through his hair, and put the hat back on. "You are wanted at the big house."

Without saying anything, I left him and headed there.

TWELVE

I SPENT the evening flipping through TV channels alone. The only light on in my house was the TV, which was dumb because there was nothing worth watching.

When I wandered into the kitchen to get a beer, a hand grabbed me out of the dark, then slapped itself across my mouth.

"Don't say a word," Dane growled behind my ear. I couldn't have. I'd pretty much stopped breathing.

He dropped his hand.

"You scared the crap—"

Just like that he placed his hand back across my mouth, and he pulled me hard against his chest.

"I said quiet," Dane hissed. "You got that?"

He released me and turned me around, and I peered at him in the dark. I nodded. He stared at me intently, his gaze sweeping from my face to my groin. It stayed there.

"Strip."

I did, shaking some as the cool air hit me everywhere. My cock didn't mind a bit though. It jumped right up when I freed it from my jeans.

Dane smiled and swiped at it with his bandaged hand. The bandage was smaller now but scratchy, which contrasted with the smoothness of the fingers that stuck out the top. The two sensations, scratchy and smooth, rubbed against my cock, making me so hard it hurt.

Dane moved both his hands slowly up my belly and chest. He pinched my nipples, first one, then the other, lightly at first and then harder until I gasped.

When I did, the pressure lifted immediately, replaced by hot, circular licks of his tongue, first to one nipple, then the other. My head spun at the difference.

I put my hands on his waist, but it was the wrong thing to do. Pinching fingers returned to my nipples. I dropped my hands right away, but he kept pinching, harder again. The pain shot straight to my cock, and my balls tightened.

How could the pain be such a turn on? Before I could think much about that, I was shifting fast from foot to foot doing my darnedest not to move or make a sound or, God help me, come. He seemed to sense that, and that I was trying to do what he said.

"Good, cowboy. Real good."

His lips replaced his fingers again, soothing away the pain as he licked and blew cool air across my throbbing buds. When he moved his good hand to my balls, fingering them softly, everything in me twitched.

He closed his hand around my cock and began to pull. My fingers grasped hopelessly at the air as I tried not to do anything that would make him stop.

I bit my lip to keep quiet. I tried holding my breath. When that didn't work, I took deep breaths. The only other sounds in the room were the clock ticking and the rubbing of his hand against me.

The pressure built, everywhere at once. I thought my head or my cock would explode.

And then he just let me go. I gasped in frustration.

"Shhh," he whispered.

Dane brushed his fingers against my jaw and nipped at my neck. "Good boy. You can make noise now, but no touching."

He dropped silently to his knees and put his hands on my waist. He dipped his head and, without warning, took me deep in his mouth. I wasn't expecting that, or anything that followed.

I exploded, cum spurting like an oil gusher. I had enough sense to push him off, so most of it hit his face, and he didn't choke to death.

"Fucking shit, cowboy," he barked, wiping his face with his good hand.

"I'm sorry. I am so sorry. I didn't expect that. Let me get a towel."

I turned toward the sink. He grabbed me hard.

"Did I say you could move?"

"What?" I stared at him, not comprehending.

He rose to his feet, towering over me. "Did I say you could move?"

I stared at his boots and realized I was somewhere way beyond naked and he was still dressed, again. I put a hand in front of myself.

"Put your hands behind your back," he commanded, his voice low and menacing. My hands were jittery as I did what he said.

He looked at me with hooded eyes. I had no idea what he was thinking, and suddenly I was more than a little afraid. *Stop this now before you lose all control. This is not good.*

But I hesitated, and he took over.

"Bend yourself over the table." He stepped aside to give me room to move, but he was still close to me. His breath brushed my ear as he finished the sentence.

"Dane, I think…." My voice was a shaky whisper.

"I said, bend over the table."

He grasped my arm and led me to it. With one foot, he kicked away a chair. With his bandaged hand, he pushed my head down onto the wooden surface and kept me there, pressing me down.

I swallowed hard and tried to push the fear away. But the voice in my head was shouting now, telling me to stop this.

My other voice whispered, "Dane, please. You're scaring me."

He lifted his hand from my head and moved it down my spine, his tongue and breath following close behind. He paused at the small of my back.

"Scared can feel good sometimes," he whispered. "Spread your legs."

But I couldn't move them. He did it instead, placing a strong hand on each thigh to pull me apart and hold me that way. Every sense I had was focused on those hands. My legs trembled.

I heard his intake of breath. He slid his good hand slowly up my leg, then up my butt, his fingers trailing in my crack. I moaned.

He rested his bandaged hand on my back, caressing my skin with the fingers that poked out.

"Grasp the other end of the table."

Something in his tone calmed me enough that I could think about doing it. I moved my arms and reached for the edge of the table, feeling the stretch and the exposure of my body to his.

He moved back slightly, like he was taking a long look at me, ass spread and arms and legs stretched wide and vulnerable. I pictured his view in my head, and my cock hardened on the table.

"Nice. Very nice."

He stroked my butt and balls and fingered my hole, and I thrust my hips toward him, begging for more. He chuckled. Laying both hands on me now, he spread my ass, then mashed it together and spread it again.

"Dane...."

"What, Josh?"

"Please."

He moved his hands away, and I heard a snap. I felt two cool, slippery fingers push into me, and I clenched against the sharp intrusion. He turned his fingers and withdrew.

"Say please again."

I wiggled in front of him like a red flag in front of a bull. "Please, Dane."

"You remember when I promised you that I was going to punish this ass?" he asked soft and low.

"What?"

"In your kitchen, breakfast, day before yesterday. You were being a smartass, and I told you your ass would be sore when this bandage came off my hand."

"I was kidding."

"I wasn't." The pause that followed was sinister. "I'm taking the bandage off now, cowboy." It wasn't a statement, it was a threat.

Goose bumps jumped up on my butt and legs, and I heard him chuckle. He rubbed his hands lightly across my skin, soothing me, warming me.

"Don't worry. This won't hurt... much."

I pushed myself up off the table to stop him. Before I could protest, his good hand hit my ass hard, first on the right cheek, then on the left.

I cried out and fell back onto the table. Dane's hands were on top of me immediately, holding me down.

"Hands back to the edge of the table, cowboy," he ordered.

"Dane...."

"Shhh. You're gonna like this eventually, cowboy. Trust me. "

He rubbed me again with both hands, taking away the sting.

"You take five more spanks—with no sound now—and I'll fuck you real good. You can do that. Do that for me. To please me, won't you?"

God help me, I wanted to, despite not understanding why, despite my fear. "Dane." I sounded like a bleating calf.

"Five. No sound now. Here's one."

I jumped as his hand cracked across me and bit my lip to stop from crying out.

"Breathe deep now, Josh. That'll help. Here's two."

I gripped the table harder and stifled a moan. Crack three came without warning. It was harder than the other two, and my butt burned. My mind raced. I thought I should pull myself off this table and order him out of my house. But my cock was weeping precum all over the table, and my balls ached to come again. They didn't want this party to end. I tried to figure how to stay silent and not bite off my tongue.

Dane rubbed my ass and back and leaned over me, his breath tickling my neck. "You're doing so good, cowboy, so good. Just two more and I'll fuck you. Ready?"

When I didn't say anything, he nipped my neck. "I asked you, 'Are you ready?'"

"Yes." I gripped the table and sucked in a deep breath.

"Good. Here's four." It was the hardest yet, and tears sprang to my eyes. "And five." Another painful smack. I whimpered.

"Shhh. All done. You did good, Josh, so good."

He rubbed my back and kissed my neck and jaw. I raised my head toward him, and he brought his lips down on mine, pushing his tongue into my mouth, plundering it. I kissed back as hard, begging as best I could for him to take me.

He pulled back, then brushed his lips softly across mine and smiled.

"Now," he whispered. He was excited, like a kid about to open a present. When I realized I was the present, a thrill ran through me. The burn in my butt was gone, replaced by an ache in my balls.

"I'm gonna fuck this red ass." He dusted his fingers across my cheeks, but the sensation went straight to my prick. "Your ass is so pretty, Josh. So red and pretty. I wish you could see." He reminded me of a horseman referring to his prize stud. I moaned.

When he ripped open the condom packet, my balls and hole clenched. He pushed in slowly, so slowly that everything, every feeling, vanished but the thrill of his cock moving in me to take me and claim me. All I could think was how much I wanted him, how deep in me I wanted him. He could have asked right then to brand me, and I might have said yes.

He kept moving forward, bit by bit, till his balls brushed my ass. I felt his cock twitch, and then he began to pull back just as slow. Need and desire clawed my gut. Sweat tickled my underarms. If he didn't speed up, I would lose my mind.

"Dane." My pleading gasp made his name a four-syllable word.

He didn't care. He moved again, in and out in the same slow motion, and I felt every bit of my inner channel like it was separate from me but just as desperate for him to ram me.

At last he did. Fast. Hard. Harder. Each thrust made my skin burn, but it was just another bit of fuel for the fire of want that consumed me. I bounced on my tiptoes to thrust back at him, and gripped the table against a feeling that I was about to fly apart.

"More," my garbled voice said from far away. "More."

Dane grabbed my shoulders and leaned over me, pinning me down, grinding my cock into the table as he thrust harder. He bit my shoulder, and I moaned and thrashed, impaled on his cock, held in place by that bite, as he bucked into me. He groaned, then froze and shuddered, his orgasm sparking through his body and into mine. I came right behind him with a loud cry, spurting into what little space there was between me and the tabletop. I clenched my eyes shut and saw stars. My heart pounded. I gasped for air.

When I could breathe again, I felt Dane's chest, heavy on me now, as he still panted hard. He nuzzled at my shoulder, and the cool sweat from his forehead transferred to my skin. My brain seemed to have merged with my cock and balls, and they were all too happy to object to anything.

Dane sighed finally and rose, leaving my back cold and goose bumpy until his lips swept my neck and then my shoulders and spine. He pulled out of me slowly and lifted me up, and I managed somehow to stand on my feet and turn into him. I wrapped my arms around his waist and pressed myself against the hard wall of his chest, kissing his collarbone over and over.

He cleared his throat, and I leaned back to look up at him. He looked embarrassed, and he gazed past my head as he spoke.

"You don't say anything about the rough sex," he said in a voice that sounded like he was strangling.

My face heated. Were we going to talk about this? After what we'd just done, what I'd let Dane do to me, I should be ashamed, humiliated even. And I was, right up until the moment I realized I'd never had sex so hot, never come like that before, and I'd do whatever he wanted to have it this way again. Even the spanking. Maybe for him it was part of the PTSD, like his nearly obsessive running and sit-ups. And didn't I just love the results of them too? But I didn't have PTSD, so was I sick for liking sex like this? I didn't want to think about it, and maybe it honestly didn't matter as long as we both liked it and no one else knew. Enough already.

"Do you like it?" I asked him back.

"Yes," he whispered, glancing away before forcing himself to look me in the eyes.

I smiled and brushed his cheek with my fingers. "Then I'm really okay with it."

He glanced at my cum puddled on the table and grinned. "I'd say you're more than okay with it, and maybe in trouble again soon, smartass. Maybe intentionally in trouble again." He pinched my butt hard.

"Hey!" But my objection was an act. I'd do almost anything he wanted to keep it like this.

THIRTEEN

IT WAS the last week of August and the last week of guests. Thank goodness. We were slammed with kids. Every family this week seemed to have six of them. I spent every day all day teaching kids to ride.

At the end of one of them, Sarah banged into my living room without knocking. My aunt had told me she was looking for me. But once I'd finished with the kids and horses and chores, I'd gone home and plopped down in an easy chair with a magazine, too tired to shower or eat or read really.

"What do you mean sending Jesse to ask me whether we're a couple?"

"Come on in." I put down the horse magazine, and she kept spitting out questions, advancing closer with each one.

"Why in the world would you do that? What was I supposed to say? Damn it, Josh. Why would you do that to me?"

I sighed. "Sarah, he asked me a couple weeks ago. I didn't know what to say. Then I thought he totally forgot about it. Honest."

"Why didn't you tell me then?"

"What happened?"

"What do you think happened?" She slugged my shoulder. "He asked me to go out with him. He's not going to stop asking until I say yes."

"He said that?"

"Yes. He told me he knows we aren't a couple, and he wants to go out with me."

"You can't," I said without thinking.

"You want to rethink that statement?"

I could almost feel the daggers she would have sent my way if she could. I blew out an aggravated breath and stood up.

"Sarah, what do you think is going to happen when Jesse finds out about me?" I started pacing my living room.

"How's he going to find out?"

"One day the two of you will be talking and he'll say something, and you'll forget and just blurt it out."

"You think I would do that?" She was incredulous. "Josh Brooks, I have kept your secret since kindergarten."

"You won't mean to, but it'll happen."

"You really don't trust anyone, do you? Not me. Not Jesse. And how do you know how your brother will react?"

"I don't know how anyone will react, Sarah. That's why I can't trust anyone." I'd paced to near her now, and I grabbed her shoulders and looked in her face, hoping to see understanding.

"I imagine Jesse will respond like most everybody would. He'll call me a faggot at best, punch me and disown me at worst. I can't afford to hope he'd be better than that. Sarah, please understand. I don't want to lose what family I have left."

She searched my face for a long while before answering, her voice softer now. "Josh, give your brother and your aunt and uncle some credit. They love you."

"They love me straight. You think you know my brother better than me? Wait—you've been spending time with him already. You're going to go out with him, aren't you?" I let go of her and turned away. "God, my life is over."

She touched my arm. "I want to," she whispered. "Your brother is a good man."

Neither of us said anything.

"Josh, you want your secret to run my life now? It's not enough that I've kept it all these years?"

She should have just stabbed me in the gut.

She started crying, and I pulled her into my arms.

"Sarah, I'm sorry. I'm just so afraid. You don't understand."

"I won't ever hurt you, Josh. I promise."

"Shhh." I rubbed her back. "I know."

I swallowed hard, kissed her forehead, and told her what she wanted to hear. I didn't want to, but I had to. "Go ahead. Go out with him."

We sat on the couch together after that until she pulled herself together. Then I walked her out onto my front porch. I glanced up and saw Jesse watching us from his. He glared at me, then turned and walked inside. Someday, I knew, he'd do that for a different reason.

Sarah headed for her car, which was parked at his place, and she smiled and waved at me before she got in. I waved back, hoping that if I acted like nothing was going to change, nothing would. But I was fearful.

OVER the next couple of days, I didn't see much of Dane, Jesse, or Sarah. Dane had finished Aunt Kate's laundry room, and she loved it and him. Now she had him working on some furniture project. Jesse and the hands were bringing in the last hay crop.

Sarah had her hands full with all the kids, and I was busy with kids and horses from sunup to sundown. Or I was trying to make myself get some sleep. It wasn't working. The conversation with Sarah was always in my mind, along with a horrible sense that something was about to blow up.

Aunt Kate finally caught on.

"Josh, you look like you haven't slept all week," she said one night as I helped her clean up after dinner. "What's the matter?"

"Too many kids?" I smiled lamely. "I just haven't slept much this week for some reason."

"What reason?"

I put on a happy face. Not like I hadn't done it before to hide things. "Nothing, really, Aunt Kate. I'll be fine come Saturday, I'm sure."

But she was still looking at me like she wasn't certain. "I'll do this. You go to your cabin and enjoy the quiet. Maybe that'll help you sleep."

"I can't leave you with all this."

"Your uncle can help me. Now shoo." She tried to look stern and waved me away with both hands.

"You're sure?"

"Go."

So I did. I headed to my place, avoiding anybody who looked like they might come anywhere near me. I grabbed a couple bottles of beer and settled in on the back deck to watch the sun go down. The wind, which had been blowing all day, had finally stilled enough so I could hear the horses near the barn and even some ravens clacking at each other across the pasture.

After a few minutes, those noises faded away, replaced by voices and images from the past. I pictured the faces of friends from college who had come out to their families. There was Andy. His parents sent him to a psychiatrist when he told them. The doctor wanted to fix him, and when Andy quit talking to him, Andy's parents quit talking to Andy. He hadn't been invited home in years. Evan's family threw him out on the street. He lived with a group of us for a while in Bozeman. We told him we didn't mind that he couldn't help with the bills, but it bothered him. He had to drop out of school, and eventually he just disappeared. Nobody knew where he was now. Todd's mom told him he was going to hell if he didn't quit acting on his "evil desire." There was just the two of them, and he quit seeing all of us. Last time I'd run into him, he was going to church, his mom was happy, and he was still worried about hell. He looked like a skeleton.

I could see myself being next on the list, losing my family and my horses, having to leave the ranch, everything I loved and the only thing I knew how to do.

"They can't find out," I whispered to myself. "No way."

"No way what?" It was Jesse, coming around the corner of the cabin.

"Jeez, you scared the crap out of me," I yelled. "Don't you know not to surprise somebody like that?"

He sat down next to me and helped himself to the other beer I'd brought out. He was smiling, like my reaction was funny.

"What you got to be scared about besides Ray Hanson, and me going out with Sarah on Saturday night?"

He grinned. I felt cold down to my bones.

"So you asked her." I tried to sound like it was fine, but I could tell by his scowl that I failed.

"This afternoon." He stared at me now, daring me to say anything. When I didn't, he added, "I'm taking her out to dinner in Livingston."

"Have a nice time." I put my bottle down and grabbed my knees to hide my shaking hands.

"It'd be nice if I thought you meant that. What is your problem with this?"

"How would you like it if I was dating or sleeping with your best friend?" Crap, I was reaching for anything, even the truth.

"For starters, my best friend is a guy."

I could feel Jesse's eyes on me. I kept mine fiercely on the worn-down peaks of the Gallatins, as different from the jagged Absarokas as I was from Jesse.

"Well, we've always been opposites, haven't we?"

Wasn't it the truth? Me, Mr. Deep in the Closet Cowboy, who cooked and had a sensitive way with horses and went into shock when our folks died. And Jesse, Mr. All-Around Macho Army Ranger. Crap, when I thought of it that way, why didn't he just know?

"Why didn't you tell me the truth when I asked if you two were just friends?" he demanded. "What game are you playing, *little brother?*" He put a lot of emphasis on the last two words.

I didn't like this conversation at all. I stood up and took a few steps just to get away from him. "I don't know what you mean."

He was in my face. "Here's what I mean. What the hell is up with you?" he yelled. "You've been leading me and everybody to believe for years that there's something between you and Sarah. But there's not, and you knew I wanted to go out with her. What kind of brother does that?"

He lowered his voice. "Why are you doing this, Josh?"

God, I wanted to scream out the truth and see what happened. I wanted to run. I wrapped my arms around my stomach to hold everything in.

"I'm not trying to do anything," I said through clenched teeth. "Go out with her. I don't care."

His beer bottle shattered against the back of the cabin, and he stomped away.

FOURTEEN

SATURDAY I stayed home. I didn't mind not seeing anybody, including Dane. He was probably getting an earful from my brother about how deceitful I'd been about Sarah. I got headaches trying to imagine his reaction.

My chance at a relationship with him had to be over. If Sarah felt like she was in the middle, Dane must be feeling that times twenty. I wouldn't want to be with someone with my baggage either. I sat in my living room, staring at nothing, feeling sorry for myself.

The knock at the door surprised me. When I opened it to find Dane, I smiled. His smile was hesitant.

"So, I thought maybe we could go for a ride and check out that fence line while the lovebirds are out."

"Great idea."

"Actually, it was Jesse's idea. He's been checking that fence every day since you found the beer cans."

I shrugged. "It's still a good idea. Let's go."

I grabbed my hat and led the way to the barn. When Dane headed for Sugarpie's stall, I told him to ride Hector.

"Who you going to ride then?"

"Hurricane."

"Are you kidding me?"

I shrugged, trying to play cool. "You spend enough time by yourself, you can get a lot done." It probably sounded like a complaint, but it wasn't, and I grinned as I said it.

"About that, cowboy…."

I was going to let him off the hook with an "It's okay," but what came out was, "Yeah?"

He dragged his hand through his hair. "It's not you. You understand that? It's me. I don't do relationships. I mean, I haven't had one."

"Why not?"

His answer was painfully slow in coming. "Couldn't. I suppose I wouldn't know what to do with one either."

"Relationships involve two people. I think that means you're supposed to let the other person help you with it."

He huffed out a breath, and his face turned grim. "I'm a loner, cowboy. But I'm not a user."

I kept my attention on cinching Hurricane's saddle, not sure how to answer. I didn't feel used, but I didn't know where I stood with him either.

"I understand."

"You don't understand," he said. "Look…."

His voice faded off, and he looked away, staring at the barn wall like he hoped some magic finger would scribble the right words on it for him.

"The last couple years, except when I've been on missions, I've run real hot and cold with everybody. It's not just you. I drove my teammates crazy. Alienated some."

He'd finished saddling Hector and was rubbing the horse's neck.

"It's part of the PTSD, I suppose," he continued. "Or maybe not. I've been doing it so long sometimes I think it might just be the way I am. It's ticked off your brother."

"I figured he was driving you nuts," I offered. "You know, with all this stuff between him and me and Sarah."

"Yeah, I've heard all I want to about that." He looked at me with some sympathy, and impatience too. Like the mess was all my fault?

"Let's go." I didn't want to hear anymore if he thought it was.

"Josh." The edge in his voice was like a command, and I looked at him. He rubbed his jaw and stared into space again. Then he looked at his boots.

"Fuck. You help me feel better. When I'm with you, okay?"

"Okay." I bit my lip so I wouldn't smile. But his statement made me feel warm all over. "Let's go for that ride."

"Yeah."

I could feel his relief from across the barn. We headed outside, mounted up, and rode into the back meadow. To my surprise, Dane kept talking.

"What was it like growing up on this ranch?"

"Didn't Jesse tell you?"

"I want to know what it was like for you."

I thought a minute before answering. "Great. I mean, I don't know anything else, you know? But I wouldn't have wanted anything else. There was a lot of hard work, still is. And it was rough when my parents died. But my childhood was great."

"I fell in love with this place hearing about it in your letters to Jesse."

"You read my letters?"

"No, Jesse read them to me. He was so happy to get them, and I didn't get any."

"He never told me how he felt about them. I just kept writing. I didn't want him to be lonely."

Dane laughed. "That's one thing your brother will never be."

"What was your growing up like?"

"My dad was in construction. I had a little brother."

Dane paused so long I thought that was all he was going to say. Finally he continued. "He had cerebral palsy like Steve Sanderson."

He looked at me, and I didn't hide my surprise. "Yeah, that's why I could relate so well to Steve. Anyway, Sam died when I was nine, and Mom left. Dad drank, and he and I moved a lot. Then I joined the Army."

"What about your dad?"

"He's still in Wisconsin. He sends me Christmas cards."

"Does he know about you?"

Dane shook his head. "Nobody knows. The Army has this thing called Don't Ask, Don't Tell. I know you know about it. You told anyone?"

"Are you kidding? This is Montana."

"But Sarah knows. And your friend Guy is out."

"Sarah told me I was gay in kindergarten, when we both admitted having a crush on Timmy Benson. She told me not to tell anybody, and she never did."

"You're kidding? She's good at keeping secrets."

"I hope."

"You mean with Jesse."

"Yeah."

He was quiet a minute, considering all I hadn't said. "I think I'd trust her, cowboy."

"I don't have much choice now."

He nodded. "What about Guy?"

"He's been out as long as I've known him. He told his parents when he was in high school, and they were okay with it. He's artsy, girls like him a lot, and he lives in a city, where it must be easier. I always envied him that."

"Being out?"

"Yeah. It would be so great to live your life the way it really is, without having to tell lies to hide that you're not going out with a girl, or who you're really going out with, or worrying that your family or people you work with will find out. But I can't risk telling."

We'd reached the fence line, and it was fine, so we turned our horses and rode a course running parallel to it on the ranch side. Hurricane was having no trouble taking commands or moving alongside Hector.

"Why aren't you and Guy a couple?" Dane's voice was even as he asked. I decided to answer honestly.

"I think Guy would like that. But he's not"—I shrugged—"the one. I love him like a friend. He knows that, and it's okay for now."

We'd crossed a large meadow and were nearing another thick stretch of forest on ranch property. In another two hours it would be too dark to be in the woods, but I didn't want to turn back yet.

I swung off Hurricane, pulled out the blanket I'd tied to the back of my saddle, and threw it on the ground.

"Want to sit for a while?"

Dane dismounted, spread out the blanket, and sat down. I unsaddled both horses and tied them to a tree, spread their blankets out to dry, and then sat by Dane. He cast a sidelong glance at me, and I scooted close and maneuvered his head into my lap. He didn't protest, so I undid a couple of his shirt buttons and began brushing my fingers across his chest.

He arched an eyebrow at me, then closed his eyes. His face relaxed and he didn't move, so I didn't stop touching, stroking his nipples, and running my fingers across his chest. I let my mind wander a bit to imagine being able to do things like this every night. Then I noticed the bulge in his jeans and let my hand wander lower.

He reacted lightning quick, like I'd bit him or something. He grabbed my hand, rose up, and swiveled around to face me before I could make any kind of move.

"Nice try," he chuckled, now gripping both my hands hard. "But not what I had in mind."

He moved up onto his knees, then rested back on his heels. "Open your jeans and pull 'em down below your knees."

He dropped my hands, and I stared at him. He stared right back.

"You heard me."

I turned a hundred shades of red, but I did it. With a few ungraceful wiggles and huffs, I maneuvered my jeans and briefs to my shins. I kept my legs together as I reclined back on my forearms, trying to look cool, but I was anxious. My cock stood up stiff, and Dane smiled.

"Touch yourself."

"This isn't what I had in mind." I didn't move. I was beyond embarrassed.

He motioned with his hands for me to get moving. "I know you've beat off at least once in your life."

"Not in front of anybody." I glared at him. Then I whined. "This is humiliating."

"Come on, cowboy. Before it gets too dark for me to see anything."

"You're serious?"

He slapped my thigh and shot me a threatening glare. "You'll feel how serious in a minute."

God help me, I remembered the spanking and how my prick got so hard and hurt so good. I groaned and closed my eyes. Tentatively, I slid one hand down my belly. I grabbed at myself and pulled hard.

Dane swatted at my hand. "I want a show, with some balls action, and commentary."

My eyes flew open, and I jerked my hand away. "Commentary? I'm not some porn star, you know." Again I was whining.

"Pretend. And keep your eyes open." He stretched himself out and leaned back to watch my discomfort.

"You're just trying to make me feel stupid."

"Don't test my patience."

I stroked across my balls with bumbling fingers, then spread my knees and let my fingers slide down toward my hole. Then, like my body had a mind of its own and it was being run by my dick, my fingers slid back and forth confidently, teasingly, across that sensitive skin.

Dane's mouth slackened and his eyelids lowered over his heating eyes. I was turning him on. "Commentary now." It was an order.

I tried to think of something, I really did. But nothing… came. When I saw him frown, fear stabbed at my stomach, and I stuttered out the first thing I could think of.

"My hand is hot and the air is cool. I'm harder than—" I stopped everything. "Aww, hell, Dane, this is stupid."

He glared at me. "Did I say stop?"

"Dane…."

"Keep going," he growled.

I swallowed hard and looked past him, and a vision of him touching me rushed into my mind. At last I had something to say. "I'm pretending it's your hand. You're touching me soft, a tickle, and I'm so hard I ache for you."

He groaned, and I looked at him and saw the flush in his face. I was turning him on. Maybe I could do this. Maybe it could be fun.

I ran my fingers up my cock, smearing my forefinger through the precum.

"I'm leaking already. I want your hands on me and... I'm leaking for you." I lifted the finger toward his mouth. "Want to taste?"

"You taste it." His voice was tight. His eyes were hungry as he watched me move my finger to my mouth and lick it. I licked my lips next, and he moved his right hand to caress his jeans as he watched.

I swallowed hard. "You taste better."

He squeezed himself, and I echoed his actions before lightly pumping myself with my fist. I arched my ass off the blanket and looked at him.

"I'd rather it was you."

He moved around beside me, and dropped his hand atop mine. He pushed hard and slid my hand up and down my cock, pulling at my skin and my desire.

My prick wept some more, and I begged. "Please, Dane."

"Undo my jeans."

I flipped onto my knees and ripped at his belt and zipper.

When I'd tugged his jeans down, he pushed me down on all fours. A second later, I heard the rip of the condom wrapper and the squirt of the lube, and then he was pushing into me. He slid in shallow, then began to pump, going deeper with each stroke. I choked out a groan.

"So good, cowboy."

He reached his hands under my armpits and pulled me up into his chest in a quick, fluid movement. He thrust into me with a grunt and slid deeper. I was sure he could feel my heartbeat through his cock.

"Dane," I begged. I had to have more.

He gave it to me. And though he held me firmly against his chest, I flopped around like a doll, his doll, and I was happy to be it. Pain melted into pleasure and became craving as I climbed up a mountain of want, so close, so close.

I squeezed my eyes shut, focused on nothing but him plugging me over and over. I could picture it as I felt him hammer into me. I clenched my gut and my ass and my fists and pleaded with him not to stop. His breath huffed warm and wet past my ear. He was like a piston, and I took it all, shouting when I came. Like he'd been waiting for that, he thrust hard once more, driving me onto my forearms and blasting into the condom. He shuddered for a scary long time after that, until his head came to rest on my shoulder and he panted against me. When he'd caught his breath at last, he kissed and nibbled at my neck.

"So damn good," he whispered.

I raised us up slightly and kissed his forearm, which was still strapped across my chest, and we knelt like that, me holding up his weight, until he began to soften.

I winced when he pulled out, and he skimmed his fingers across my back.

"You going to be able to ride back?"

"Just give me a minute." Even if it hurt like hell, it'd be worth it.

He rose up with a groan, then reached out to help me up. He didn't let go until I'd wiggled my pants back into place. He pulled up his own, kissed my shoulder, and turned toward the horses.

When I'd zipped up, I turned to face him, expecting he'd be saddling Hector already. But he hadn't moved.

"Cowboy," he whispered. "We're being watched."

FIFTEEN

"WHERE? What should I do?"

"At normal speed, like you're not aware of them, let's saddle up and move out. They're near where the fence problems have been."

"How—"

"Reflection off binocs. I don't know how many guys. Now pick up the blanket, and let's move toward the horses."

I did as he said, setting my pace to match Dane's and mindful the whole time that he was putting himself between me and whoever was watching us.

"Lead us out of here without any backtracking. Can you do that?"

"How fast?"

"Whatever's normal."

Yeah, right. What's normal when you're imagining a target on your back and a high-powered rifle pointed at it?

"We really shouldn't go too fast, because of the bad light. Horses could step in a hole."

"Then go slow. And look for a way to get a hill or trees between us and them."

We set off, Dane always behind me. After what felt like forever but was more like fifteen minutes, he moved Hector even with Hurricane and me.

"It's okay. We're out of sight and range. Head for home."

"Who could it be?" I asked, though I knew Dane had no way of knowing. I had to talk about it, maybe to shake off the fear. He seemed to understand, because he began figuring out possibilities with me as we made our way up and down the hills toward home.

"Jesse discovered the downed fence right after I arrived. And you didn't have any problems before that, right?"

"Right. None."

"So what else happened around then? Anybody pick a fight with anyone on the ranch? Anything new or different happen?"

"I got Hurricane just before you arrived."

"That's it?"

"Yeah."

Dane didn't say anything.

"Hanson? You think…."

"He's a possible. He's been awfully interested in how you're doing with this horse, even showing up when he's not wanted."

"What do we do?"

"I'm thinking."

He didn't say anything more. I focused on getting us home without incident as the horses walked in and out of shadows and near blackness. I knew where we were, but for the first time in my life, I wished I'd left a light on at home. Steering for it would have eased the jitters in my gut.

At the barn, Dane handed off Hector without saying a word. I led the horses inside and took care of them. I had no idea what Dane was up to. When I left the barn, I still didn't see him.

"Well, crap. He just went off to bed?"

"No, he's checking your perimeter."

Dane's voice came from close by, and I jumped. My heart pounded in my ears, and the fear was back, gripping my belly.

"Jeez, like I haven't been scared enough already tonight?"

"You can relax. No one's around." He emerged from around the side of the barn. "But you can see this barn, the corral, and your cabin from where they've been watching."

"Great."

I went inside, turning on every light switch as I made for the kitchen. Dane followed. I got two beers out of the fridge, and we sat down at the table.

"What do we do?"

"We'll talk it over with Jesse and your uncle tomorrow. Meanwhile, I'll spend the night here."

"I'm not arguing, but why?"

He took a swig from the bottle and swallowed. "Because I can kill people with my hands, and you can't."

I WAS sitting on my bed in the dark when Dane got out of the shower. "So which'll be easier for killing people, the bed or the couch?"

He pushed the door open wider and came toward me. "I'll take the bed."

"Okay then." I got up to head for the couch. I didn't want to; Dane was naked. But I didn't think he'd want to spend the night sleeping together, not after what happened the last time. And I didn't want to ask and get rejected.

He grabbed my arm as I passed. With a hard push, he drove me to my knees.

"How about you put that smart mouth to better use." He stepped close so his cock was in my face.

Okay, I could get into this. It would keep my mind off things too. I palmed his balls. He threaded one hand through my hair and stroked my chin and cheek with the other, and I forgot about my fear.

He was damp and smelled like my soap, but there was only a clean skin taste as my tongue swept across his balls. He widened his feet and sighed.

"Cowboy," he whispered, "I could get addicted to you."

I was good with that.

SIXTEEN

DANE and I went to Jesse's early. He wasn't up yet.

"Must have been some date with Sarah," I muttered as I put on the coffee.

"It was," Jesse snapped, rubbing his eyes as he walked into the kitchen barefoot and bare-chested. The only thing he'd managed to put on was his jeans.

"Hey, Josh meant that in a good way. Didn't you, Josh? In fact, we're over here so he can make you breakfast."

I began pulling out pans. "I hope it was a good date, Jesse," I said. My stomach was flipping like a pancake, but I was trying to be sincere. "Was it?"

Jesse leaned his butt against a countertop, glaring at me before he turned to frown at Dane.

"And what were you doing sleeping at my brother's again last night? People are going to talk."

Oh crap. What had Sarah said? I flashed Dane a panicked look. He ignored me.

"We're here to talk with you about that," he answered calmly, taking a seat at the table. "How about some coffee, Josh?" He gave me a look that said just calm down.

"Got it." My voice sounded like a high-pitched cartoon mouse to me, and I cleared my throat to cover it up. I opened a cabinet and grabbed three mugs, then poured the coffee and took two of the mugs to the table.

"You want eggs or pancakes, Jesse?" I was concentrating on taking deep breaths now, and I thought I sounded almost normal.

"Can you make that egg pie thing with bacon?"

"Egg pie thing?" Dane asked.

"It's a quiche. But Jesse thinks 'that egg pie thing' sounds more manly." Honestly, could I sound more gay?

"Just make sure it tastes good," Dane said.

I rummaged through Jesse's freezer for the pie dough and broccoli.

"It's a good thing I stock your freezer."

"Maybe you won't have to much longer," my brother replied.

"So the date went that good?"

"Yeah, no thanks to you."

"Okay, let's keep this friendly. You"—Dane glanced at me—"just concentrate on making breakfast. Jesse, Josh and I went riding near the downed fence line last night, like you asked. Fence was fine, but someone was watching us."

"What?" Jesse straightened up in his chair.

"I spotted a reflection off binoculars. They were right by where you repaired the line. We were a half mile off. Did you know you can see everything about Josh's place from up there, including where he trains Hurricane?"

"You think whoever downed that fence is watching Josh train that horse?" Jesse was fully awake now and sounding skeptical. "But why?"

"Good question," Dane replied. "How many folks know about that horse?"

"Josh, you haven't been talking at Cunningham's, have you?"

"No," I snarled, not turning from where I was mixing up the quiche. "And see if you get breakfast if you keep implying I'm an idiot."

"Enough," Dane said. "We got a problem, remember?"

He turned back to Jesse. "Josh hasn't been talking up Hurricane. But who's overly interested in how he does with that horse?"

"Hanson. But that doesn't mean he's spying."

"But when did this fence business start?" Dane asked. "What else was going on? Who has a beef with Brooks Ranch?"

"Nobody's got a beef with us. And nothing was going on… except that Josh bought that damn horse."

"It isn't my fault." I let the oven door bang shut to emphasize my point. Neither of them paid attention.

"What you thinking?" Dane asked my brother.

Jesse wrapped both hands around his coffee mug and studied the liquid inside. "It's a logical conclusion, but we can't go making wild accusations."

Dane nodded.

"After breakfast," Jesse said, "we'll go talk to Uncle Karl."

The "we" didn't include me, and I felt like a little kid. I served the manly men their quiche and went back to my house.

I HADN'T been back at the cabin more than ten minutes when my phone rang. It was Sarah, and she yawned before she said anything.

"Must have been some date." I was trying harder than I had with Jesse to put a pleasant tone in my voice.

"It was the best, Josh," she sighed. "Your brother is… so romantic. It was very special."

"Great. I mean it."

"I know you do. Did you see Jesse yet this morning?"

"Yeah. I made him breakfast."

"That was sweet, Josh. So?"

"So he liked it fine, I think."

She huffed, and came back at me so loud I had to hold the phone away from my head. "Josh Brooks, you know what I mean. How did he seem?"

"He seemed like he had a real good time too."

"Oh good." She sighed and was quiet for a bit.

"So did he ask you out again?"

"Yes, but I couldn't give him particulars yet. School's just beginning and I have a million things to do. But Josh, we didn't talk about you."

I apologized again for asking her not to go out with him. She told me it was okay, and we hung up.

Had I been an idiot to worry? It looked like the worst that would happen if they got serious was that I'd be stuck in the middle of their gooey goings-on until Sarah really did start stocking his freezer.

TWO hours later, I was working in the big horse barn when Uncle Karl came looking for me.

"Let's talk," he said, motioning me to the bench near the tack room door and waiting until we sat down to start.

"Jesse and Dane came to see me with their idea about what's going on with the fence line."

"Does it make sense?"

He shrugged. "There's no way of knowing yet, but Ray Hanson comes from a long line of competitive men prone to doing stupid things. His dad went to jail once for knocking out a man who simply talked to Ray's mother. Then when she divorced him and wound up with Sam Milford, there was a lot of vandalism at the Milford ranch for a while. Folks wondered whether it was Ray or his dad, but nothing was ever proved either way."

My uncle tipped his hat back. "There's nothing we can prove now either. But I want us to be careful. For the time being, I'm going to ask you to keep Hurricane in this barn and avoid riding anywhere near your house or that fence."

"What is it with Hanson and me and horses?"

Uncle Karl didn't say anything right away, like he was mulling something over in his mind.

"Do you remember any of the ranch hands around the time you got Pokey, Josh?"

"No. I was only about four," I reminded him, "and the world was pretty much Mom and Dad and Jesse and Pokey and you and Aunt Kate for me." I couldn't imagine where this conversation was headed.

He nodded. "Ray Hanson worked for us briefly then. He even stayed here for a bit."

I was stunned, but my uncle merely nodded and continued.

"He was out of high school a couple years, and he and his dad had had a fight. His dad kicked him off their ranch. Ray fancied himself a horse trainer already, and of course your dad was the best around. Anyway, we hired him on, partly to help Ray out."

No one had ever mentioned any of this, and it didn't seem to me that Jesse could know it either.

"He was only here a few days when he and your dad got into a disagreement about training methods, as you can imagine. Ray wanted to physically fight your dad about it. I guess that's the way they handled disagreements on the Hanson ranch.

"Your dad wouldn't, and when Ray pushed it, your dad let him go. Ray's dad took him back after what we heard later was a really brutal fight between them. Most people think Ray won because he began running the Hanson ranch around that time. He's run it ever since."

My uncle rubbed his jaw. "This whole time, that incident didn't come back to me until Dane and Jesse told me what Dane saw yesterday. And I can't say there's anything we could have done if I'd thought of it sooner. I'm still not sure the two incidents are related."

"I understand."

He blew out a breath. "But I think Dane's idea to stay at your place for a few days is a good one."

I should have been happy, and the part of me below my belt was already cheering in its own embarrassing way, but I really didn't like the implications.

"I don't need a babysitter, Uncle Karl."

He smiled. "I know you can take care of yourself, son. Just like I knew the day you brought home that horse that you'd do what Hanson couldn't."

My uncle didn't hand out praise often. I smiled and nodded. "Okay then."

He nodded back. "The Hansons don't fight fair. Remember that, Josh."

"Yes, sir."

Uncle Karl was ready to change the subject. "So, now that that's settled, we're having dinner at the big house around five. Dane and Jesse will be there. You come too."

"I'll come early to help Aunt Kate."

He smiled. "I was hoping you'd say that."

SEVENTEEN

SO DANE came to stay at my house that night, and everyone was glad about it.

Dane, Jesse, and I watched a baseball game at Jesse's first, and Jesse and I behaved like there was nothing wrong between us. I felt like he had something left to say about Sarah, but he wasn't ready. Maybe he'd just forget everything if they finally became a couple. Or maybe Sarah would be able to smooth it all out. She was good at things like that.

When we got back to my place, I headed to the bedroom right away. I was removing some of my clothes from a drawer when Dane walked in.

"What are you doing?"

"Making some drawer space for your things." I dropped a pile of shirts on the floor of my closet and turned around with a grin, but Dane wasn't smiling.

"I don't need drawer space." He pointedly dropped his bag in a corner. "I won't be staying that long."

I swallowed my embarrassment and disappointment both. "Okay then. Umm, what about sleeping arrangements?"

"Make up the couch like someone's sleeping there, but rough up the blankets to make it look like I just got up. I'll sleep in here with you, but it will mislead anyone good or bad who comes in."

I grinned. "Sounds great."

When I returned to the bedroom, he was sound asleep. I guess I missed the part where he was serious about sleeping. I slipped under the covers without disturbing him, but I was awake and bothered for a while.

THE next morning started out as bleak. I woke up with the world's biggest hard-on, but Dane wouldn't budge as I tried to wake him up just by calling his name. I'd learned my lesson about touching him while he slept.

When he opened his eyes at last, he pretended not to notice my condition. He rolled over to face me and gave me a kiss, and then another. Then, he was kissing me lots more, soft kisses mixed with deep and hard ones. It was real nice, but I got more frustrated by the minute as he avoided every one of my attempts to put his hands on my cock.

When I'd squirmed and moaned enough for five orgasms, he finally gave me a "Poor baby," and beat us both off. Then he rolled over me, pinning me to the bed.

"Wasn't that worth the wait?" He was grinning like he'd accomplished something major.

"You are a terrible tease."

He gripped my arms harder. "But it was worth it, wasn't it?"

I huffed out a breath. "Yes. And I like waking up like this."

He chuckled and kissed my cheek. "Good answer. Now what are you making me for breakfast?"

Over pancakes, we talked about what we had to do that day and agreed to meet at Jesse's to watch the football game that night. I even said I'd make dinner.

Dane helped me clean up the dishes and then headed for the door, but he turned around before opening it. I thought maybe he meant to kiss me again, but I was wrong.

"Remember. If anybody asks, I slept on the couch."

THAT night, Uncle Karl joined the three of us for part of the football game. A couple of nights later, Jesse and Sarah joined Dane and me for dinner when she came over to tell me about school and Jesse noticed her car, dropped in, and wouldn't leave.

Sarah didn't seem to mind, and neither did I. I was too busy imagining how great it could be if Dane lived with me full-time.

The nights were cooler than normal, like winter might come early. But Dane and I figured out ways to fight off the chill without turning on the heat. He came up with a game that kept my ass plenty warm and a little bit sore, and made me think about sex pretty much around the clock. I found myself liking the roughness as much as Dane. I wasn't sure why, and it embarrassed me some, so I didn't talk with him about it. Instead, I decided to just enjoy it, along with us being a secret couple right under everybody's noses.

Nothing new happened around the ranch, and my only worry was that our playing house was going to have to end soon, before someone realized it wasn't all about keeping me safe.

AT THE end of the week, Uncle Karl, Jesse, and Dane took off for an auction, so I joined Aunt Kate for lunch at the big house.

We spent some time talking about the meals that had been our best for guests over the summer and what we might change next season before she got around to what she really wanted to talk about.

"So, Sarah is dating Jesse now. How do you feel about that?"

"I question Sarah's taste," I tried to joke, "but other than that...."

"A lot of people thought you and Sarah were a couple."

"People think lots of things."

"Don't play games with me, Josh," she said sternly. "I'm trying to figure out what's going on with my nephews and whether you're okay with it. And look at me while we're talking about this."

I wanted to throw up everything I'd just eaten. I wanted to get up and run too, but I knew things would get a lot worse if I did either one. How much should I say? What would be safe?

Seconds seemed like hours as I tried to figure it out. I knew my aunt was expecting me to say something soon, but I wasn't coming up with any words. It was like my brain had slowed with the time and nothing I could do would speed it up.

I forced myself to look at her, and she was simply waiting, with a patient, encouraging look on her face.

I took a deep breath. "Sarah and I weren't a couple."

"You never have been," she offered.

"Yeah." I didn't realize then how much I was revealing. I was just trying to come up with something to say without saying much. My gaze returned to my hands on the table in front of me.

"I never paid any attention to what anyone else thought about our friendship. Neither did Sarah. But I guess Jesse thought we were together, and he's been mad. You probably realized that."

She nodded when I looked up at her, still encouraging me to keep talking.

"He thinks I've been intentionally deceiving him. But I wasn't, Aunt Kate. I'm hoping he gets over that."

"He will eventually. But how do you feel about them being together, Josh?"

"How I feel shouldn't matter."

"It matters to me." The stern tone was back in her voice.

"I wonder if our friendship will change, I suppose."

"And I suppose Jesse feels some of the same with all the time you're spending with Dane."

The thought hadn't occurred to me. "Jeez, Aunt Kate, talking about this out loud, the whole mess sounds childish."

She smiled and leaned closer, like she was trying to hold me up while leading me in the direction of coming up with good answers too.

"Childish might be harsh. Things get complicated when deep feelings are involved." She patted my hand. "I just don't want friends or lovers to come between my two boys. And you two don't want that either, not after all you've been through together. Now, why don't you take off and enjoy the rest of your day, and see about getting together with Jesse and Dane and Sarah tonight?"

I got up and kissed her cheek. "That's not a bad idea."

"Have a good time," she called as I headed out the door.

I couldn't reach Jesse when I called him, so I left a message telling him and Dane to meet me at Cunningham's a little after six. I did the same with Sarah. After I finished working some horses, I decided to head out a little early to meet them. Stupidest thing I've ever done in my life.

EIGHTEEN

I GOT to Cunningham's about five thirty. The bar was already half-full. It looked like Billy was going to have a good night.

I slid onto a barstool, ordered a beer, and pulled out my phone to call Jesse. The phone hadn't even rung yet when Hanson's voice came at me from behind.

"I didn't realize you serve faggots here, Cunningham," he said loud enough to be heard over all the other noise in the bar. All I registered was "faggot" and then the sudden absence of any voice in the bar save Hanson's, and Trace Adkins's coming from the jukebox.

"You know," Hanson continued, "I really don't think you should be in here with decent folks, faggot."

I swiveled the stool around and slid to my feet. That put Hanson's forehead three inches from my chin, but he wasn't backing up or backing down. Of course not. He had Mel Evans and two other men behind him.

"Yeah, I know, Brooks. You think you could keep that a secret forever?" His spit hit my jaw as he thrust his chin closer to my face. "Pretty soon, everyone will know all about you taking it up the ass and liking it."

Fear shivered up the back of my neck, making the hairs stand up, as I confronted Hanson's mouth. Suddenly, he seemed to be all mouth, large like a gaping black hole threatening to pull me into violent ugliness while all around the bar beyond him, stunned faces focused in on us. People I knew, people I didn't. Some disbelieving, some already disgusted. Everybody watching us. Seeing me clear but not a glimpse of that ugly threatening mouth. All of them waiting frozen, but Hanson going to spring into action any second. I knew I should do something. I just couldn't think of what, or a thing to say.

Billy Cunningham started talking though. "Hanson, you stop this bullshit, or I'm calling the sheriff. You hear me?"

"It ain't bullshit, Cunningham," Hanson replied. "Question is, is Brooks going to admit it? Is he going to tell all these folks who've been sending him their horses to break and their kids for riding lessons that he's not to be trusted with animals or kids because he's queer as they come?

"That's right." Hanson turned now to talk to the bar at large. "You all thought he had a special touch compared to me. Well he's touched all right."

His tone made me want to melt into the floor. But he wasn't done.

"Do you want a faggot around your kids? Or your animals?"

He turned back to me. "What's the matter, Brooks? You a chickenshit too, or just not talking because it's true?"

I didn't have a comeback. All I could think was that I'd been outed by Ray Hanson of all people, and what would my family say, and where was I going to have to move to.

"I think he's scared, boss," Mel Evans sneered. "He's scared because he knows the real men around here are going to show him what we do to faggots who act like they're better than us."

"There'll be no fighting in my bar," Billy yelled. "Hanson, you and your men get out of here."

Immediately, Hanson turned on Billy. "You want to throw me out, Cunningham? How much business do you think you'll get when folks learn you're throwing out real men but letting cock-sucking queers drink at your bar?"

Billy surveyed the crowd, then looked at me with anger and contempt.

"That's enough," he yelled. "I won't have this shit in my bar. Get out of here, both of you, and Hanson take your men with you."

Billy pulled out the baseball bat everyone knew he kept behind the bar and waved it at us. "And none of you come back, you hear me?"

I stared back at him, unable to believe he was ordering me out too. Yeah, I'd imagined the worst if people ever found out about me, but I never thought they'd turn on me right before my eyes. I went to school with Billy. He'd offered me a job more than once. I'd hugged him at his dad's and his mom's funerals both.

"I said out, Brooks," he hissed. "I won't hesitate to call the sheriff on you too. Believe me, I won't."

I wanted nothing more than to be out of there. If only I could make my feet move.

"You first, faggot," Hanson taunted. "I don't want you anywhere near my ass."

He shoved my arm, and I had to right myself fast. It was enough to clear the fog in my brain, and I began to walk, looking at nothing but the door. Hanson's men parted as I passed, but not without a shove or two of their own. I barely felt them.

I made it through the door, then was vaguely aware that it didn't slam behind me. That should have told me something, but I was too focused on getting to my truck.

The first blow came across the back of my shoulders. The bar door slammed right after. I stayed on my feet but crumpled in half. A punch to my side spun me around. I pulled myself up and took a swing at the first guy to step in front of me, one of Hanson's men. He fell at my feet.

A punch from behind sent me sprawling over him. I landed on my knees in the gravel, and that was it for me. I became one of those punching dolls that keeps bobbing up, only to get smacked down again.

Evans threw most of the punches. They were hard ones to my stomach and ribs. Hanson went for my face. He was responsible for the cut over my eye and the blow that had me spitting out bitter-tasting blood.

Someone kept calling me a faggot. And I thought I heard my brother far off calling my name. But that was impossible.

Then somebody, thank God, yelled, "I'm calling the sheriff." Hanson and his crew disappeared in a haze of slamming truck doors and spinning wheels.

I pulled myself up from the gravel onto my knees and wiped the blood out of my eye. I could see people watching me, but nobody came to help. I was just as glad. Maybe I still had some pride if I could get to my truck myself.

Pain like I couldn't believe shot through my ribs and gut when I stood up tall. Made me suck in a hard breath, and crap but that made everything hurt worse. Evans had done some major fist-dancing across my torso. I'd be all black and blue before morning.

I fought myself to keep my arms from gripping my gut. Made myself walk to my truck with them at my sides, like John Wayne and Clint Eastwood both. It was a long, blurry, painful way, costing more pain to get the door open. For the first time in my life, I grabbed the grip handle on the ceiling and pulled myself in. The motion made my ribs scream till I thought I would die. My butt hit the seat with a thud that rocked my ribs again, and I laid my head on the steering wheel and pulled the door shut. After a couple tries, I got the key in the ignition and took off. Luckily, it was a straight drive out onto the road, no backing up. I couldn't have turned around to check behind me for anything. I had to focus hard to keep between the yellow lines. A mile down the road, the sheriff passed me, lights flashing, heading for Cunningham's.

When I got to my cabin, I parked parallel to the front porch. I had to rest my head on the steering wheel for a bit before I could even think about opening the door. Then I fell out. It wasn't intentional, but it seemed to make things easier, at least at the start. I didn't feel any new pain until I landed on my hands and knees in the gravel drive. Then I felt everything throb all over again, plus new pangs in my palms.

As carefully as I could, I pushed myself up once more. I don't know how long I leaned against the truck before I got my feet moving and staggered to my front door. Thank God there was no one around to see me.

Once inside, I locked the door behind me. And not just it. I went round the whole place slowly, checking windows, locking them, and pulling down shades. Maybe I'd just stay behind them forever.

Much later, after I'd decided that even if any of my ribs were broken they weren't piercing a lung and my face didn't really need stitches, I slid into bed.

I hurt too much to think about what to do next, beyond figuring it might be easier and smarter to leave all my clothes on. I had this feeling I wasn't going to wake up by myself. It'd be at least tomorrow afternoon before my aunt and uncle would hear what had happened and maybe come looking for me. But two former Army Rangers might want to pound me too, one to protect his secret, one to protect his pride.

NINETEEN

IT WAS dark when Jesse and Dane woke me up by turning on all the lights in my bedroom. Only one of my eyes would open, and I saw four of them to start. But I knew it was dark outside.

"Have I been asleep for a whole night and day?"

"No, asshole. It's taken us a couple hours to find you," my brother said too loudly. I put my arm across my head to kill the light and the noise, but it didn't help that or the pounding in my head.

"You found me. Now get out of my house."

"If you weren't already beat to shit, I swear, I'd do it to you myself."

When, I wondered, was my brother going to quit yelling?

"Yeah, I'll come looking for you when I can get up."

"Shut the fuck up, both of you." Dane was angry too, but at least he wasn't yelling.

"Do you need to see a doctor?" he asked.

"No. Now, really, get out of my house, please. And how'd you get in anyway?"

"Oh no, you son of a bitch," Jesse spit out, still too loud. "I do not get an earful from half the damned crowd at Cunningham's about you being a fucking faggot and hear you get beat up over the fucking phone and not get an explanation."

I tried to rise up and was immediately sorry, but I stayed there, propping myself up on my elbows. "You heard it over the phone?"

"You called me," he snapped. "I kept calling your name."

"That explains it. I need coffee."

"Were you drunk?" Jesse yelled.

"Heck no. I didn't even get a beer before I got thrown out."

I swung my legs out, but I stumbled when I stood up, and Dane reached out an arm to steady me. His hand felt warm and comforting.

"Thanks." I couldn't bring myself to look at him.

They followed me to the kitchen, where I turned on the light, lurched to the counter, and opened a cupboard. I thought I was doing pretty good until I dropped the can of coffee.

"I'll make it," Dane said. "You sit."

He steered me to the table, pulled out a chair, and sat me down, then started making coffee.

"I can do it. I'm sore, and out to half the valley by now. But I'm not drunk."

"So it's true. You're a goddamn faggot."

I looked into my brother's face and stared until I could see him clear. For a second, he was thirteen again and holding me while I cried at our parents' funeral. Then he was in his Ranger uniform, holding me at the airport the day he came home for good. He was the one with tears in his eyes, exclaiming about how I'd grown. But I blinked, and now he was glaring at me like I made him sick to his stomach.

I didn't look at Dane. Wouldn't let myself. I pulled together all the courage I had, looked Jesse straight in the eye, and answered.

"The word is gay. You want to hit me for it, you have to wait a couple days."

Jesse slammed his fist into the table. A cracking sound exploded in the air, but the table held together.

"All that time," he huffed. "All that goddamn time I thought you were going to marry Sarah, and I loved her and did nothing."

I watched my hands, gripped in my lap, as his volume increased.

"You lying, fucking faggot son of a bitch."

Each horrible word hung in the air by itself until he spit out the next one. Then they all flew around the room together.

He jerked my arm hard, and I looked at him. I said nothing. Multiple emotions flashed across his face, until something like contempt settled in his eyes. He shoved me and let me go.

"You fucker. You are not my brother." He stomped out, banging the door behind him.

Dane put a cup of coffee on the table and slipped my cell phone next to it. Then he followed after Jesse, closing the door quietly.

I stared at the new crack in my table and my blood on the phone and drank down the coffee.

WHEN I woke up again, it was past noon. Since no one had come looking for me, I figured Jesse made sure my chores were covered.

At three o'clock, my phone rang. It was Sarah. I let it go to voice mail. She called again at four and at six. I still didn't answer.

No one came to my door. I turned on the TV, but nothing was loud enough to fill the sick empty feeling inside me.

IT WAS the middle of the night when my ribs woke me up. Falling asleep in an easy chair isn't a smart thing to do when your ribs are still trying to find their proper places again.

I began thinking back on everything, replaying the bar scene and the fight a hundred times. Now I had smarter comebacks, and I threw a few more punches. Why hadn't I managed that when it counted? I'd best them all next time. Then again, if I stayed in my house for the rest of my life, which was looking pretty appealing, I wouldn't have to worry about next time.

What I couldn't figure was why Dane hadn't sneaked over to check on me.

His secret was still safe, I was sure. Neither Hanson nor his crew knew Dane well enough to recognize him that night in the meadow. And Jesse hadn't figured it out, or Dane would be over here already because Jesse would have tossed him too.

Or did Jesse not mind that Dane was gay, but me being so was disgusting? Jesse had always looked up to Dane, and they were close as brothers, closer sometimes. Still, how could Jesse throw me over and not do the same to Dane?

And how could Dane allow it? Why didn't he stand up for me?

The thoughts went round and round, making me feel like crap and keeping me awake, even though I tried to shoot them down like the yellow duck targets of that rifle game Jesse and Dane played at the fair in Billings.

And crap, but that had me thinking back on those first times Dane touched me, and how he touched me after that, until my head spun and my cock started up a conversation all its own and neither one would stop. I about cried when it occurred to me that it was all over now for sure.

I got up and made coffee and just wandered around my cabin drinking it and trying to shut myself up. I think I walked five miles by the time the sun came up, and I didn't have any better thoughts. I was just more miserable.

I DRAGGED myself outside real early and took care of Hector, Hurricane, and Sugarpie. Turned them all out to pasture.

As I came out of the barn, Jesse was headed in my direction. When he saw me, he turned around and walked back into his house.

I sat in mine the rest of the day. I didn't look at myself in a mirror. Didn't look at much of anything.

But I finally came up with an idea about Dane. He wanted to stay in the closet, so he had to avoid me. Anybody associating with me would be tagged as gay or a sympathizer.

When I considered why I hadn't heard from my aunt or uncle, my only thought was that they were ashamed but didn't want to tell me. I wasn't their son after all. Maybe I wasn't even their nephew anymore. I was going to be another of those poor gay bastards who lost their family when their secret became known.

I didn't let myself wonder too much whether my parents would be ashamed of me too. I'd always imagined that my mom, who I thought made over me a little bit more than she did over Jesse, did it because she knew the truth, even when I was little. I'd read that about moms. I thought it was maybe her way of trying to prop me up for what would come. I couldn't handle thinking she might hate me too. It felt too much like digging my fingernails into a scabbed-over wound that had never really healed.

At last, I listened to Sarah's voice mails. First one, she was worried. Second one, she wasn't talking to Jesse anymore. Great. Another reason for my brother to hate me. There was no third message. I guess she'd finally given up.

I waited until dark before I went out again to take care of the horses. Then I came back and sat in my living room in the dark.

TWENTY

"DID you want to say something, or just stare at the poor queer?"

I don't know how I became aware that Dane was standing in the hallway between the living room and bedroom. He hadn't made a noise. I just felt him there.

"Wanted to make sure you were okay."

"I am. But please don't turn on a light and see for yourself."

"Can I come in?"

"Seems strange to ask since you already are. In, I mean."

"I'm sorry, Josh," he said from the hallway. Guess he was going to stay there.

"Don't be," I told the darkness. "Your secret's still safe, right?"

"Yeah."

"I'm glad." I really meant that. "How's Jesse?"

Dane didn't answer right away. "Madder. Sarah won't talk to him."

I wondered what he was leaving out. It was quiet a long time. "You still there?"

"Yeah." He sighed. "I don't know what to say, Josh. I don't know what to do."

"Nothing you can say or do. Just take care of yourself. You don't want to be where I am."

A minute later, though I never heard a sound, he settled his hand on my shoulder, and I let myself sink into it. It felt so good having somebody with me, somebody touching me.

"Get up."

He was in front of me before I'd gotten out of the chair, smoothing his hands up and down my back real gentle to keep from hurting me.

He brushed his lips over mine, soft so as not to hurt.

I needed more. I pushed my tongue into his mouth, heading deep for his throat, and he let me. I grabbed his shirt and yanked it out of his pants. I needed him touching me everywhere.

But he gripped my hands and stopped me. I pulled my tongue back in my own mouth.

"Who's in charge here?"

I pressed my forehead into his shoulder. "You are."

"Lose the shirt and pants."

I shuddered, but I stepped back and started to remove my shirt. He helped me some when I winced, and he helped me take off my boots and pants too. Then he walked away to sit on the couch.

"Come here."

I moved to stand in front of him, and he ran his fingers lightly along my bruised ribs. His warmth seemed to heal every place he touched.

Without warning, he stopped moving his fingers and swallowed my cock. I rocked wildly, surprise making me nearly dizzy, and he grabbed my ass hard and tight. His tongue flicked across me fast and insistent, sliding and licking, while his mouth just kept up the suction. I closed my eyes and gave myself up to it, alternately gripping and petting his hair as he made me crazy.

"Gonna come."

He pulled off me, and I slid to my knees so I could kiss him. I poured all my feelings into it. He stroked my back, then held my jaw and pulled me close as he returned the kiss, deep and long and loving.

"Please, Dane, fuck me face to face." It was out without my thinking, and I couldn't take it back. We had never done it that way. I sensed it was too bare for him, like he'd rather skip the condom than do it that way.

He stilled but didn't let me go. He sat me on the coffee table, rose and took off his clothes, then tossed a condom beside me.

"Lie back on the table."

I smiled.

"We still do this my way."

"Of course." But the smile didn't leave my face.

When I'd settled on my back, he leaned over me. I raised my head to kiss him, but he pulled back.

"Spread your knees."

His gray eyes were dark as they swept my body, and I splayed my knees wide and wanton. He sank between them, his weight settling on his arms to protect me, his steel-hard shaft rubbing against mine. Slowly he lowered his head to one of my nipples, licking it first, then nibbling and biting down hard. When I gasped, he soothed it with his tongue.

I rubbed my hands against his sides in a futile attempt to make him grind on me. He grabbed them and pressed them to the table above my head. "My way," he hissed.

I surrendered and lay still. He ground his cock against mine, the friction wonderful but nearly unbearable too. I wanted to come so bad. I shut my eyes as I concentrated on the contrasting, building sensations.

He slipped the condom on and pulled my ankles toward his neck, raising my ass off the table as he pushed deep into me.

"This what you want?"

I opened my eyes wide and nodded furiously, afraid to say anything that might make him stop. He might never do this again.

Like he could read my thoughts, he smiled. "That's right," he sighed as he pulled back and slid into me again. But was he answering me or echoing how it felt? I didn't know.

I tried to pull him deeper inside by clenching all my muscles. He quirked an eyebrow at me, then dropped his hands on either side of my chest and pushed hard. I hooked my ankles over his shoulders in a desperate attempt to hold on and grasped wildly at his arms as my desire sparked higher.

"Fuck, so good, cowboy." Pleasure moved across his face until his eyes slammed shut and his jaw tightened.

I groaned back at him, a sound that went on and on, louder and louder until it was a shriek.

Dane's eyes popped open. "Not yet. Don't you come yet."

I whimpered. I was going to shoot any second. He knew it too, and grinned wickedly. I clenched with everything I had to stop myself from exploding, and that sent him over the edge.

"Come with me," he gasped.

I shot before he'd finished saying "come." In that instant, all the pain and hurt left my body as I spurted across my stomach and chest and his too. I knew the moment he felt it because he sighed. He laid himself softly across me, and I buried my face in his neck. I tasted the salt of his sweat and felt him tremble as he held himself off my battered ribs.

Eventually he eased off me. His eyes were closed. His face had softened, and a tiny smile played at the edges of his mouth. I realized in that moment that he meant everything to me. That despite what had happened to me, I was happy for that.

He opened his eyes, and it was like he could read the thought on my face. His smile faded, replaced by a grimace of regret. Every part of him tensed. He pushed away from me, grabbed his clothes up, and started to dress.

I scrambled for my pants and put them on too. We didn't look at each other.

"I gotta get back."

"I understand."

But I didn't.

TWENTY-ONE

ANOTHER day passed, and I saw no one but the horses. Once, I saw Dane running, off in the distance. Jesse was still avoiding me. I guess my aunt and uncle were too. Sarah wanted to come over. I told her not to.

But I needed to talk to somebody. I decided to go to Bozeman. I didn't look so much like Frankenstein anymore, though it's not like most Montanans haven't seen a beat-up cowboy before. I figured it'd be okay.

I went straight to Guy's. The gallery was open, but he had a customer inside. I tried his back door, but it was locked. I returned to the front and pulled my hat down low as I walked by the gallery windows and kept going for a couple of blocks. Crossed the street and came back. Crossed the street and walked by again. The customer was still inside.

How pathetic could I get? And when was someone going to call me out for loitering?

I was about a hundred feet past Guy's front door when he called my name.

"Come on in, Josh. You think I didn't notice you?"

I turned around and kept my head down. "I didn't want to bother you with a customer."

"Silly. I'll just be a few more minutes." He held the door open for me, and I kept my head turned away. "Go through and head upstairs. I'll join you in a few minutes."

I slipped by without Guy getting a close look at my face, and I nodded to the stranger without looking up. Once upstairs, I sat in Guy's kitchen to wait. About fifteen minutes later, I heard him on the stairs.

"I put the closed sign up," he said as he shut the door to the stairway. "So what brings you to—Oh God, Josh, what happened to your face?"

"It's nothing."

"Like hell." Guy had his hands all over my shoulders, tilting my neck this way and that to look at me. I winced when he accidentally brushed my ribs.

"You tell me everything right now, or I will have one hell of a hissy fit."

I pushed back my hat, and he grabbed it off my head and put it on the table.

"You got anything to drink? Pop, maybe?"

He got me one from the fridge, and a bottle of water for himself, and sat down next to me. I took a long drink.

"You remember that horse trainer I told you about? Ray Hanson?"

"The one who sold you the mustang."

I nodded. "Turns out he was hiding out near my place and watching me train Hurricane, and saw some more besides, you know, between me and Dane."

I played with the pop can so I wouldn't have to look at Guy. "Anyway, Hanson outed me in Cunningham's, and then he and his men beat me up in the parking lot."

"Where else did they hurt you?"

"You mean besides my pretty face?" I tried to grin, to keep things light, but I had to stop when my lip threatened to break open.

"Did you go to the doctor? Did anyone help you?" Guy asked. "I hope Jesse and that Ranger kicked their asses."

"No."

Guy's face darkened. He took my hand. "What's happened?" he whispered.

"Jesse's furious and he's not talking to me. Neither are my aunt and uncle. Dane's got to protect himself. His secret's still safe."

"Oh Josh." He bit his lip and squeezed my hand. Lightly, he brushed my sore lip with his fingertips. He genuinely hurt for me.

"Have you heard from Sarah?"

I shook my head. "She's called, but I haven't gotten back to her. I'm afraid I've totally wrecked things between her and Jesse."

I pushed my chair back and rubbed my hand across my forehead. It was one of the few places on my face I could touch without hurting.

"Is Jesse mad just because of that or because…."

"He said some ugly stuff."

Guy jumped out of his chair and began to pace the kitchen. "That stupid jerk. Doesn't he realize how lucky he is that you're his brother? Doesn't he remember all those letters you wrote him when he was in Afghanistan, all three times he was there? Shit, I bet you wrote him every day. I'm going to call him and blast him but good—wait a minute." He stopped fast and pivoted to face me. "Why aren't you angrier about this?"

"What do you mean?"

"You know exactly what I mean. You haven't said a bad word about any of them. You haven't even raised your voice."

"There's no point. First off, you know I don't like to get mad and—"

"Fuck that," he shrieked. He could become pretty hysterical when he wanted. "This is something to get angry about, Josh. These people are abusing you."

"They're just mad. They think I've kept something I shouldn't have from them, and they're right."

"Right?" Guy was screeching now. "Who you sleep with is none of their business. Don't you defend them. I won't stand for it."

"Or what, Guy? Nothing anyone can do will change anything. This is my life for a while."

"This happened, what, four days ago? What have you been doing since then?"

He bounced from one subject to the next like a wild shot on a pool table. I took a deep breath and let it out. Took another.

"I've been pretty much staying in my house, letting my face heal up."

"Oh Josh." He flopped back in his chair and grabbed my hand again.

"You can't hide this away, darling. You have got to face them all, your aunt and uncle, Jesse and Sarah, and that coward in-the-closet Ranger—"

"Watch what you say about Dane." I was surprised at the anger in my tone.

"What?" Guy's voice went up an octave. "Now you're upset? At me?" His face reddened. "What the fuck's the matter with you, Josh? The Ranger's not saying a word to defend you. Won't even come out of the closet to help you. And your family has you hiding in your house. You going to stay there forever? The closet wasn't enough?"

He wasn't going to stop. I tried to flatten my voice to keep from amping him up some more. "I told you, Dane has to protect himself. Leave him out of this."

Guy jumped up again. "Fuck Dane," he yelled. "Why are you protecting this guy?"

"Because I love him," I shouted back.

And didn't that surprise us both. Guy slumped in his chair.

"You love him," he said slowly. "Well, isn't that just a kick in the gut."

He shook his head and closed his eyes for a long moment. When he opened them again, he looked in my face. "What about me? I've loved you for years."

"Like a friend. I know that, Guy, and I appreciate it. You know I do."

"Oh no," he spat out. "Do not patronize me. Do not belittle me. I *really* love you. I've loved you for years. I've been waiting for you… to love me back." Tears filled his eyes.

"Guy," I whispered. I reached for his hand, but he jerked away. "You're one of my closest and best friends. I love you as a friend. You know that. You know that's how I've always felt."

I looked at him expectantly, searching for understanding. Evidently, everybody I knew was fresh out.

Tears spilled onto his cheeks. "I've been waiting for more." He looked hard at me. "Get out. Get out of my house and don't come back."

I stared at him, expecting his outburst to dissipate like smoke, believing he'd take it back and ask me to stay. But not today. How had he failed to understand? What had I gotten wrong?

I got to my feet. I felt like I should say something, but I didn't know what. I left without looking back, an uncomfortable feeling in my chest. I pushed it deeper inside with each step down the stairs.

Outside, it was raining now, hard. Seemed about right. Seemed things couldn't get much worse.

I was wrong about that too.

TWENTY-TWO

IT WASN'T raining at the ranch. The afternoon was perfect, cool and sunny with puffy white clouds scattered across the blue big sky.

I needed to do something. I headed for the barn and saddled Hurricane. No reason I had to keep him hidden now. What else could Hanson do to me?

Even though Hurricane didn't want to, I kept our pace slow to protect my ribs. As we made our way through the back meadow and the fence along the national forest line, I grew accustomed to the occasional jabs of pain. Pretty soon I didn't notice them or where we were going.

My mind played over the events of the past couple of days again, adding the disaster with Guy, skipping ahead, rewinding and replaying without much logic. With no answers. Just lots of recriminations. How had I missed Guy's true feelings? What could I do now?

Thunder halted my thoughts. I looked up and hard rain peppered my face, like the sky was spitting on me too. The storm had followed us from Bozeman after all. Crap.

I slowed Hurricane and paused to look around. Low clouds had moved in with the rain and closed down the view. I couldn't see the mountains on either side of the valley. I saw the grass right around us and nothing but a whole lot of gray beyond that. But Hurricane must have been paying attention. We were back along the national forest fence line, not too far from home.

Lightning flashed, followed by thunder too close by. Hurricane pranced nervously.

"It's okay, boy. We'll go home." I patted the side of his neck, wiping off a sheet of rain as I did. My clothes were soaked.

I turned him just as the thunder cracked again. But it wasn't thunder. It was three loud noises back to back to back. Something heavier than wind rushed by me.

Hurricane fell suddenly to the ground. Pain that shoved the wind out of me shot through my chest as we both hit the dirt hard. Neither of us moved for several minutes. I couldn't breathe and my ribs ached like nothing I'd felt before.

For too long, I struggled to get air back into my lungs. I felt lightheaded and shaky as I lay still taking stock. I couldn't figure what had happened. I tried to get up, but my leg was stuck under Hurricane, and he wasn't moving. His breathing was irregular too.

I got my arms under me and pushed myself to a sitting position—God, did my ribs hurt—and ran my hand down Hurricane's neck. It came up dripping red liquid. I stared at it, not comprehending anything except that it wasn't rain. I unzipped my jacket and wiped my hand on my pale blue shirt and it turned red, too, the huge red blotch seeping onto my undershirt.

It was blood, it had to be blood. So much blood.

Like that, my head cleared. The sounds, the rush of wind, the blood. We'd been shot at, and Hurricane was hit. Not only that, I'd turned my horse into the bullets.

"Oh, God, no. No, damn it. No!"

My horse was shot, and it was my fault, and we were stuck here. I fell back on the ground, and I shrieked when the pain wracked my ribs again. But it was nothing like the pain in my heart.

Right on top of that came a scarier thought. Were we safe? Where was the shooter? Even as I pressed myself flatter to the ground, I glanced around as much as I could. The bullets had come from behind us, from the area where Hanson and his men had cut the fence.

Hanson. He must have fired the shots.

Lightning flashed again, like a cosmic agreement, and something broke open inside me.

"Hanson, you mother-fucking coward," I screamed. "Come fight me now, damn you. I'm ready."

But he was gone. I was sure. He was too much of a coward to stick around. I turned back to my horse.

"Hurricane, come on. We have got to get up."

He thrashed his legs and grunted, but he didn't rise.

"Please, Hurricane. You have to try."

Once more he struggled but didn't succeed.

"Okay, boy, I'll go get us some help. But you have to help me get up."

I pushed on his back and tried to move my leg.

"Hurricane, help me, please. I have to get up to get you some help."

I patted his side, and he tilted his head in my direction. Then he rocked himself slightly, enough that I could pull myself out.

"Good boy, Hurricane. Good boy. You rest now."

I patted his neck and got more blood on my hands. God, there was so much of it, pumping out of a ragged hole in his neck. There was a second wound in his shoulder.

I ripped off my jacket and shoved it under his nose to keep it out of the red-streaked puddle of blood and rain growing around his head. Then I took off my shirt and pressed it into the neck wound. I used my T-shirt to gently plug the smaller hole in his shoulder.

"I'm going to get help. Please, Hurricane. Don't you leave me too."

I pushed myself onto my feet, grabbing my ribs against the pain, and started stumbling for Jesse's. Faster, my mind cried, but my body was slow to respond. Not even the icy rain that stabbed at my bare back and chest could speed my feet. The terrifying thought that I wouldn't get help in time brought tears to my eyes.

"God... please...."

After a quarter mile, I spotted Dane and Jesse coming toward me, with Uncle Karl's truck behind them and closing. I pushed myself to get to them, my breath coming in gasps.

Jesse stopped once he was close enough to get a good look at me.

"What the fuck happened now?" he yelled.

Dane ran up and grabbed both my arms. He was staring at my chest. When I looked down, I was painted in blood, some of it thinned by rain and spreading down my pants.

"Are you hit?"

"You heard the shots?"

He shook me hard. "Have you been hit?"

"It's Hurricane. He's hit. I turned him right into the bullet. Oh, God." I was sobbing now, and I didn't care if Dane thought I was a coward. "We have to help Hurricane. Hanson tried to kill my horse."

Dane gripped my arms harder, and I wanted to throw myself at his chest so he would hold me. But I couldn't. I knew he wouldn't.

"You're not hurt?" he asked again.

"No." I clutched at his arms. I had to make him move, make him do something fast. "But we have to get back to Hurricane."

He took off his jacket and threw it across my shoulders. "You first. Put this on before you freeze."

Uncle Karl walked up to us. He held the jacket as I slid my arms into it. "You're okay?" he demanded. Jesse still kept his distance.

I nodded and grasped at my uncle now. "We have to get back to Hurricane. He's been shot in the neck. Please, Uncle Karl, you have to help him." I swiped at the tears on my face.

"Jesse, get us a trailer, and bring my operating kit out of the calving barn. And call your aunt. Tell her what's going on and have her call the vet."

Jesse and Dane took off at a run, and Uncle Karl and I jumped in the truck. My uncle gunned it, but still, everything seemed to take too long. I beat on my knees with my hands, trying to speed us up as I stared out the windshield watching for my horse.

Uncle Karl spotted him first, and I flew out of the truck as soon as it stopped. I dropped to my knees alongside Hurricane's head. He moved slightly in my direction, like he was reaching out for me to comfort him. I rubbed his jaw and forehead.

"Uncle Karl will fix you, boy, I know he will."

My uncle squatted down in front of Hurricane, rubbing and soothing him as he surveyed the wounds.

"Damn, I wish I could tell how much blood he's lost. Obvious neck wound. And one in his front shoulder."

He touched both my shirts but didn't pull them free.

"Good job, Josh," he said, his eyes never leaving my horse. He probed with gentle fingers until Hurricane thrashed.

"There now, boy. You stay calm for me, okay? But Hurricane, we need you to get up."

"He tried twice already, Uncle Karl, and couldn't."

"Maybe if we get him some traction under his feet. Go see what you can find in the truck, son."

I ran to it and ransacked my way through the capped bed, tossing things every which way until I found some burlap sacks. I grabbed them and ran back to my uncle.

He was still inspecting Hurricane's neck wound.

"How bad?"

"I can't tell."

"You're not lying to me?"

"No, Josh. I wouldn't." His words kicked me in the gut. I turned away from him.

"I'm sorry, Uncle Karl. Really."

He stood up and put his hand on my shoulder, then turned me toward him. "Nothing to be sorry about, son. I think I understand. Now, get those spread out under Hurricane's feet, with more under the back feet. He's gonna shift his weight real fast once he feels the pain in the front."

I did as my uncle instructed.

"Tell your horse to get up, Josh. You can make him do it."

I uncinched the saddle, then stepped away to give Hurricane room to move. Making sure he could see me clearly, I held out my hands. "Hurricane, get up now."

He looked at me and raised his head.

"That's it. Get up. Hurricane, get up."

After several hard huffs of breath, like he was priming himself, Hurricane rocked off his side. His feet thrashed under him, then found the burlap sacks and planted firm. His muscles clenched and quivered, and he squealed when he put weight on his front legs. But he kept moving, kept pushing, and rose to his feet. With a dull thud, the saddle slid to the bloody red ground.

I threw my arm across his back and fell on his withers, hugging and patting and praising him, but staying far away from his wounds. "Good boy, Hurricane. You're going to make it now, I know it."

Uncle Karl walked around him. "Well, we've got one exit wound. Looks like one bullet went clear through his shoulder. Do you know how many were fired?"

"Three."

"Then there could be two in his neck."

"No. One went past my head." As I said the words, I knew they were true, and I realized I could have been hit too. I clutched Dane's jacket around me to stop the shakes that suddenly interfered with my ability to talk.

Anger like I'd never seen clouded my uncle's face, and he clenched and unclenched his jaw. Then his arm went round my shoulders and he pulled me close, trying, I guess, to warm me up. But he was shaking too.

"H-Hurricane...." My tongue kept hitting my teeth, and I couldn't say anymore.

"I don't know for sure, Josh. Damn it, where is your brother?" He tightened his hand on my shoulder, and he scanned the area Jesse should come from. Then he looked at me again, his anger pushed aside by his concern for me.

"It may look a hell of a lot worse than it is. Neck wounds can be that way."

I nodded. I knew he was trying to keep me hopeful, and I wanted to believe him.

We heard the truck then, and it appeared moments later. When it came to a stop close by, Dane and Jesse jumped out, leaving the doors open and the truck running.

"Vet will be at the hospital before you, getting stuff prepped," Jesse said to Uncle Karl. "He says for you to call and update him on your way."

"Josh, load Hurricane up."

I did as directed and came around to the cab.

"You drive," my uncle instructed me. "I'll stay in back with Hurricane and call the vet."

I climbed into the driver's seat and then stopped. "Hurricane's saddle?"

"Got it," Dane said as he slammed the passenger side door. "Get going."

I DROVE as fast as I could to Livingston, passing cars whenever I could and keeping an ear out for noises from the trailer. But Hurricane was quiet. When we arrived at Doc Russell's office, I pulled around back. He already had the large door open for us.

Uncle Karl jumped out of the trailer and made for the vet. I brought Hurricane out, careful to avoid the pool of blood on the floor, and we went into the clinic.

The vet tech, a brown-haired girl who'd been a few years behind me in school, already had the room prepped. She fiddled with a tray of instruments rather than look at me.

Doc Russell didn't give an indication of anything when he saw the wounds. He just pointed us toward the waiting area out front and led Hurricane deeper into the clinic.

My uncle took a seat on a hard plastic chair in the tiny space between the dog and cat food display and a rack full of pet toys, collars, and dental chews. The lights were off, and the room was darkening as the sun set.

I sat in an identical chair across from Uncle Karl and stared at the white linoleum floor. I pictured Hurricane's head in the bloody puddle, and the blood on the trailer floor, and the vet tech who wouldn't look at me.

"You don't suppose…." I began without thinking through what I wanted to say.

"What, Josh?"

I looked up to see my uncle looking at me with sympathy.

I cleared my throat. "You don't suppose he won't try real hard because I'm gay, do you?"

Uncle Karl closed his eyes and shifted in his chair, then opened his eyes and leaned forward toward me.

"I'd been hoping we would have spoken a couple days ago, son, but you didn't come see me." It wasn't a rebuke. He sounded sad.

I glanced around the room, making sure the vet tech wasn't around.

"The doc will do the best he can, Josh, like he's always done for us. Nothing's changed."

My uncle leaned toward me, so less than two feet separated our heads, and continued softly. "Now, let's have this talk we could have had years ago."

I nodded and stared at the floor again. I gripped my rain-soaked jeans.

"I've been waiting since I heard what Hanson said in the bar. I finally decided maybe you were too embarrassed or ashamed."

I nodded and chanced a look at his face. He was struggling to find his words. I waited.

"I never realized you were gay, Josh," he said, confusion and sadness flickering across his face. "Your aunt says she thought maybe, but it never occurred to me. And I'm not happy to hear it."

My whole body froze, bracing itself.

"But it's not for the reasons you think," he continued. I guess he'd seen my reaction.

"When your parents died, I promised them at the funeral that your aunt and I would take care of you and Jesse like you were the children we were never able to have."

He looked down at his hands clasped in front of his knees. I looked at them too. They were scarred hands, with a finger that wouldn't bend anymore and faded marks from cuts and rope burns and stitches across the wide tanned backs. They were strong hands.

He cleared his throat. "We tried our best to do that, and I don't think we let you down."

"You didn't do anything wrong."

He searched my face. "I'm glad to hear you say that. So, I'm hearing this about you and remembering back over all these years. Your parents didn't do anything wrong, that's for sure. And now you tell me Kate and I didn't, and I accept that."

I nodded and waited.

"I started thinking about all I've seen in cattle—the females that will mount each other, and the bulls that mount females and males. Did you know that some male sheep won't ever mate a female, but will mount other males? Bill Green told me that once when I was visiting his operation."

I glanced at him, and he nodded to emphasize his point.

"Anyway, what I'm saying, I guess, is that some animals seem to only like their own sex, and I always figured that was just the way of nature sometimes."

"Yeah."

"So it must be nature when it occurs with people too. I can't reason anything other than that, given my experience. And other people can tell me they believe different, but I'm going to decide based on what I know."

He reached out one of his hands and laid it on mine. "Josh, your aunt and I are sorry this is how you are—"

I winced and looked away.

"Look at me, Josh," he said sternly. "I want to be sure you really understand what I'm saying to you. This is important."

He squeezed my hand hard, like he could force my compliance, I guess. I pulled my eyes back to him.

"Thank you." He released my hand, swallowed, and continued. "We're sorry you're gay, but only because we know it is going to make life extra hard for you, because of how people can be. You already know that, I guess, after what Hanson's done and what other people are saying. And maybe that's why you never felt you could tell us yourself."

He paused again. "We wish it could be different for you because we love you, Josh. And I wish there was something I could do to make it easier, but there isn't, and I hate that. Do you understand?"

I nodded, and tears welled up in my eyes. I blinked them back hard and looked at the floor. I was too close to crying again.

"Now your aunt, when she talks to you, will probably say a bunch of stuff about the grandchildren she won't have. She's always said your grandchildren would be special."

He smiled briefly, then looked incredibly sad. "We've never told you or Jesse how hard it was on her when we didn't have kids, and I won't. But remember that if she says anything about grandkids, all right? And try to understand what she's really saying."

I nodded. "Thank you." It came out in a muddled whisper. It was all I could manage.

He frowned, and his forehead wrinkled like it did sometimes when he couldn't understand what someone was saying.

"Nothing to thank me for, son. This is what family does. This is how love behaves."

I tried taking in everything he said, I tried real hard. I'd underestimated both him and my aunt, and I was ashamed.

"I'm sorry."

He patted my knee. "Don't be. I'm just sorry you thought it was a secret you had to carry alone."

After a minute, he stood up and stretched. "Damn, I hate waiting like this."

He walked around the shelves, to the front door and looked out the window.

"You want anything from Bridgers across the street?" he asked.

"A beer?"

He grinned. "Maybe a celebratory one when we get home."

"Yeah. Good idea."

He came back and sat down again.

"Do you think Hanson was aiming for you or the horse?"

I was quiet a moment before I spoke. "Hurricane, I think. But why'd he go that far? It wasn't enough, what he did in Cunningham's?"

My uncle shook his head. "I've been trying to figure it myself. He just couldn't stand you besting him and had to erase the proof, I guess. But Josh, I don't think there's a lot we can prove legally."

"I know." I sighed. "It's okay. I don't care about Hanson. Even if Hurricane doesn't make it," I gulped, "nothing'd be enough to make up for it."

He nodded, and we sat together in silence as the room got dark and the neon lights of the bar across the street came on and illuminated the waiting area.

TWO hours later, Doc Russell came out.

"Geez, Karl, you could have turned on the lights."

"What's the word, Dave?" my uncle asked.

The vet turned to me. "I think he's going to be okay, Josh."

All my muscles relaxed. I hadn't realized how tight I'd been holding them. Even my hands hurt. The vet was still talking, and I concentrated on listening.

"One bullet went clean through his shoulder, and I was able to remove the one in his neck. I've cleaned everything out real good. He'd lost a fair amount of blood, but if an infection doesn't set in, he's going to be fine. We'll have follow-up med and wound care, and some down time. But I think he's going to be fine."

Doc Russell gave me a big smile.

"Can I see him?"

He nodded and motioned for me to follow.

TWENTY-THREE

UNCLE KARL drove back to the ranch and headed right for my cabin. As we got out of the truck, Jesse's door banged, and my brother and Dane headed toward us.

"Well?" Jesse asked my uncle.

"Looks like Hurricane is going to be okay. Dave is real hopeful."

"Good," Jesse said. "You're sure it was Hanson?"

Even though the question wasn't for me, I answered. "Who else? Came from the same spot where the fence was wrecked. Same spot where Hanson was when he spied on me."

"I don't see how we prove it," Jesse said, turning pointedly toward my uncle.

Uncle Karl watched us closely. I knew he picked up on what Jesse was doing, but he didn't say anything.

"Josh and I agreed to let it go," he said.

Dane spoke up. "I should have been able to prevent this."

"You couldn't have," Jesse insisted.

Dane shook his head. Later, I would remember that and realize he was shaking me off too. "I should have," he repeated.

"It's okay. Hurricane's going to be okay." But Dane didn't seem to hear me.

"I'm leaving," he said loudly. He stared into the dark above all our heads. "I got a call. I'm leaving."

Jesse and my uncle didn't say a word. I couldn't believe what he was saying.

"You can't leave. Not now. I love you."

Dane winced like I'd kicked him.

"Oh, fuck," Jesse spat.

Dane glanced at Jesse for the briefest second, then turned toward me and looked over my head.

"I love you." I grabbed at Dane, but he took a step back from me.

"I told you not to."

I froze inside. Everything in my mind, in my vision, tunneled down to only Dane. I didn't see anything but him moving away from me. I couldn't think of anything but him leaving.

"Don't go. Please, Dane. Forget what I said. I didn't mean it. I take it back. Don't leave me." My words came out in a rush that ended in a barely audible plea.

He turned to walk away.

"You can't do this," I yelled at his back.

He kept walking.

"Only cowards walk away."

"I'm already gone." He barely turned his head as he tossed the words over his shoulder.

"You fucking coward," I screamed, clutching at my stomach. "Go to hell."

Still Dane didn't turn around. He didn't say anything. Jesse followed behind him, not talking, just following. And I realized he already knew Dane was leaving.

I didn't look at Uncle Karl, but I knew he stood in the drive watching the two of them walk toward Dane's truck. My vision blurred, and I ran into my house and slammed the door shut.

Tears ran down my cheeks. I slid down the door until my butt hit the floor. Sobs broke through my clenched teeth, and I shoved my knuckles in my mouth to force the sound back down my throat. My whole body shook.

I heard Dane's truck start up and pull away, and I stilled. I stopped breathing, straining to listen. When I couldn't hear it anymore, I gasped in a breath and started sobbing for real, over Dane and Hurricane and Guy and how Jesse felt about me.

After a while, it hit me that Jesse didn't seem to mind that Dane was gay. It was clear he didn't consider me his brother anymore. But he wasn't bothered at all about Dane.

The truth of that stabbed me like a gut punch, and a pain too sharp to name melted together with my tears. I covered my head until the tears finally stopped, then clutched at my aching ribs.

Shit, I still had Dane's jacket on. I ripped it off and threw it across the room. If I'd had any energy, I'd have burned it. But I didn't. I wiped at my nose with the back of my hand. I got up and moved to the couch, where I curled up in a ball and stared at the damned jacket, cursing it and Dane both.

When I became too cold, I got up and put on a shirt. As I came back into the living room, there was a knock on the door.

"Can I come in?" Uncle Karl called.

"Yeah." I wiped at my face with the tail of my shirt.

He let himself in and headed straight for the kitchen, the smell of my aunt's beef stew following after him. Even though I wasn't hungry, I did too.

"Sit." He pointed to the kitchen table. I slipped into a chair. I hung my head so he couldn't see my swollen eyes or the tearstains. Then again, did I really have anything else to hide from him?

He put a cloth-covered steaming bowl in front of me, then brought me a soup spoon from a drawer.

"Eat." His eyes didn't leave my face.

I stared at the bowl. The stew topped mashed potatoes, just the way I liked it. I scooped up a spoonful and swallowed.

"Keep eating."

He went back to the cupboard and located two glasses, then got the milk out of the refrigerator. He poured some into each glass and set one in front of me, then sat down across from me. He watched me until I ate everything in the bowl and downed the entire glass of milk.

"Good," he said. Finally, he took a long drink from his own glass.

"I'm sorry Dane left. Sorry for both of you. I don't think he's as sure of himself as he wants us to think."

He was quiet a minute before he added, "We can hope he comes back."

I nodded.

"You get some sleep now, Josh. Then come have breakfast with your aunt and me tomorrow, and we'll go see Hurricane."

I nodded again.

He stood up. "I know you don't believe me and this doesn't help at all right now, but things will get better. You believe that, son."

I nodded and got up. I didn't believe him, but I didn't want him to know. He'd been so understanding about everything, I couldn't let on that I doubted him again. I ducked my head. He settled his hand on my neck and pulled me into an embrace. He held me for several minutes.

"We'll get through this together, Josh."

I nodded. When I finally let him go, he reached for the empty bowl.

"I'll wash that and bring it in the morning."

"Oh no," he said, holding it away from me. "You can't deny me the happy look your aunt is going to give me when she sees you emptied it. See you in the morning."

I DIDN'T leave the ranch for days after that, except to visit Hurricane. Then he came home, and I didn't leave the ranch for another week. I spent most of my time with him, caring for him or simply talking to him. Uncle Karl had one of the hands take care of the rest of the horses for me.

I didn't see Jesse the whole time. I ate most of my meals with my aunt and uncle, and he didn't join us. To be fair, he was moving cattle part of that time, from the mountains to winter pastures closer to the big house.

I made it through the days, but the nights were long, full of bad thoughts and painful memories. My bed felt too empty. I missed Guy and my brother. But mostly, I ached for Dane.

Sarah came over one afternoon to see me. We went for a walk past the cabins, around the swim pond, and through the woods. It was cool, and a stiff wind signaled winter's approach. But the sun was bright and warm and healing.

I filled her in about Guy and Dane, and she stopped walking and hugged me close.

"I'm sorry, Josh. Do you think they'll come around?"

I shrugged. "I don't even know where Dane is or how to get in touch with him. But Guy... I hurt him bad, Sarah, and I didn't even know it. I wish I could do it over."

She laid her head on my shoulder. "Guy is overly emotional. It makes him a good artist, but it can be hard for the rest of us. Give him some time, maybe?"

"I hope, but I'm not so sure." I changed the subject. "So how are your classes this year?"

She smiled and took my hand and steered us back toward the pond. It was her favorite spot on the ranch. "Like always. A couple really good. A so-so one. There are some great kids in my writing class, including one boy I know is gay."

She looked up at me, shading her eyes against the sun. "Do you think I should tell him it's okay to write about it, and I won't tell anyone?"

I smiled. Sarah's gaydar was good, and she always wanted to help her students. "You probably ought to wait to see if he knows it himself. Some of us don't have friends who point it out to us in grade school, you know. And some guys don't figure it out until long after high school."

"Okay." She was quiet a long time.

"Have you talked to him?"

"Who?"

I chuckled. "My brother. Mr. 'He's So Romantic'."

"Was romantic," she corrected, venom in her voice. We had reached the pond, and she headed for a bench under the trees and plunked down. I sat beside her.

"Sarah, he's a good man. Don't let what's between him and me get between you two."

"Always so forgiving. Never angry, Josh?"

"I try."

"How do you do that?"

"Aw, Sarah...."

Folks had asked me that question before. She knew that, and that I didn't like talking about the subject. I just wouldn't. But I had to do what I could to make sure she didn't stay mad at Jesse because of me.

She was studying my face now, like she could hear my inner debate.

"Come on, Josh."

"You remember the day my parents died?"

"Of course."

I knew she did. I was called out of class to hear it from the principal. Sarah told me later that the secretary who sent me to his office whispered the news to my teacher as soon as I left the room. Sarah heard, and the next thing anybody knew she was running down the hall right behind me. She slipped her hand in mine and went in that office with me and heard it too. Held my hand the whole time until Uncle Karl arrived to pick me up. Held my hand a lot during all the time I didn't talk to anyone after, even though I didn't talk to her either.

"I got real angry at my mom that morning, Sarah, and look what happened."

She stared at me a long time, like she was remembering back and trying to figure out what I meant.

"You know those two events weren't connected, right?"

"I do now, I guess."

"That's why you quit talking."

I nodded.

"What do you mean when you say, 'I guess'?"

I smiled. "Is this Teacher Sarah about to lecture me?"

She took my hand and grimaced back, but her eyes were smiling. "No."

"I know what you're going to say," I began, hoping to make myself clear and end this conversation fast. "And I agree with you. My anger did not cause the accident. But the last time I saw my mom, I was angry at her. And she knew it. Yeah, I was little then, but I was nasty. I said ugly things that I can't ever take back. Now I'm grown up, and I understand cause and effect. But I don't ever want to have anything like those feelings again. I don't ever want my last conversation with anybody to be an angry one if I can help it."

My last words to Dane came back to me in a painful flash, and I buried them fast and deep, along with the shame stabbing at my heart. They rang through my head every night in the middle of the night, for a long time, always followed by a smartass voice telling me it was too bad I hadn't learned anything from that mistake after all. I was living again with a lot of feelings I thought I'd left behind in childhood, feelings of regrets you couldn't make up for and self-hatred that didn't fade in the morning light.

I gripped Sarah's hand hard. "I don't want that for you with Jesse, ever. Do you understand? And I don't want to be the reason for it either."

"But I am angry with him about how he's treated you and what he's said."

I swear, if she'd been standing right then, she'd have stomped her foot like she used to when she was little. "Jesse and I will get past this, Sarah. We're still brothers. But it may take a long time."

I knew that in my heart. Or maybe I just couldn't bear to think we wouldn't be close again.

"But this division right now between you and Jesse is really about me, not something related to the two of you. And it's not right or fair to him that this should end your relationship."

"We were hardly together long enough to be a relationship," she scoffed.

"He's loved you for a while. He's known you long enough, and himself long enough, for the words to be true. Don't be quick to throw that away."

"But what if he's an antigay bigot?" she demanded.

"We both know he's not." I realized I knew that was true. "A lot of his anger is about him believing all that time that you and I would get married, Sarah, and that I'd been dishonest with you too. Does that make sense?"

"I suppose."

"I swear, if you were five again, you'd be sticking out your tongue right now."

She punched me and wiggled into my side so I'd put my arm around her. "When'd you get so wise?" she asked.

"Please, give him another chance."

"Just for you."

"That'll do. But don't tell him that's the reason, okay?"

She smiled and slugged me hard.

A few minutes later, we both got up. She took my hand, and we headed toward my place. As we got close to Jesse's house, she slipped her hand out of mine and walked toward it.

I went home and stood behind the curtain framing the front window, where I could see out without being seen.

About twenty minutes later, they came out of the house together. He was smiling. He walked her to her car and opened the door for her. They didn't kiss, but she touched his arm before he closed her in, and she waved to him as the car started down the driveway. He waved back and stood there looking after her long after her car disappeared.

I slipped away from the window.

TWENTY-FOUR

A COUPLE of days later, my aunt came looking for me in the big horse barn. In a panic, I dropped the tack I was checking.

"What's the matter? Is Uncle Karl hurt?"

She laughed. "It's nothing like that. I've decided that today is your big day to reappear in society."

I didn't like the sound of that one bit. "What do you mean?"

"I need to go shopping in Livingston, and you're coming along to help."

"Since when do you need help shopping?"

"I'm stocking up for winter, and I need muscle to push the cart."

"You are making this up."

"Nope," she said with a wicked twinkle in her eye. "Now go up to the big house and wash up. We're going to town."

"Aunt Kate…."

"You cannot hide on this ranch forever. And I'm still as able to put folks in their proper place as I was when you quit talking." A broad smile spread across her face, making her fine wrinkles disappear.

"I really need to get this tack fixed, Aunt Kate."

"And I really need your help in town. Now go clean up."

"Oh, no! It's Killer Kate!" I teased, like I had when she'd pushed me right after I started talking again. Back then she was so happy she let me call her that.

"You know I paddled Jesse's behind the one time he said that to me."

"You're kidding?"

"Nope. And he never forgot it. Was the last time he sassed me. Now get moving." She smacked my butt as I walked past her and out the barn door.

ONCE the truck got closer to Livingston, I started thinking the whole idea was a bad one, especially when we drove by the grocery.

"There's a couple things your uncle wants from the hardware store. Thought you could help me get them," she explained.

"Sure."

The grocery, I figured, would be loaded with women this time of day, and they'd likely limit their disapproval to nasty looks. Those I could handle. But the hardware store would be full of guys, especially old guys. My stomach soured.

Aunt Kate patted my thigh. "It's going to be okay, Josh, no matter what happens, I promise you. I've been reading about this on the PFLAG website. We are going to be surprised at who is supportive and who isn't, but we're going to get support. You believe that."

I kept my mouth shut. The only thing I believed was that I'd become her new project, and I wasn't pleased.

We walked into the hardware store and faced our first test at the door. Behind the counter was Bob Granger, and he was talking to Mr. Campbell. A retired rancher, Bob was a valley old-timer. But he still had the lean frame of the rodeo competitor he'd once been.

Mr. Campbell was an old friend of my uncle's. He took one look at us and turned his back. Mr. Granger frowned at him and looked up at me.

"Hey there, Josh," he said, friendly like always. I nodded.

"I was really sorry to hear what happened to your horse, son," he said. "Glad you weren't hurt."

"Thanks, Mr. Granger. Hurricane's getting better every day now."

"I'm glad," he said sincerely.

"Hello, Art," my aunt said to Mr. Campbell.

He didn't say a word. Didn't turn around. My aunt frowned.

"Hello, Kate," Mr. Granger answered.

"Bob." She smiled. "Guess us Brookses are going to learn who our true friends are."

Mr. Granger eyed Campbell sternly, like he was giving him a second chance. But Campbell ignored him too and fiddled with his purchases.

"I'm real sorry, Kate," Mr. Granger said. Maybe he thought being in charge of the store meant he needed to apologize for rude customers. "You'd think people who'd known you their whole lives would just take everything in stride," he added.

"Some people can't help it, I suppose," my aunt answered.

That was it for Mr. Campbell. He grabbed his things and stomped out of the store. I guess we won that one.

My aunt handed me her shopping list and pushed a cart in my direction. "Will you go find these things for your uncle, Josh?"

I bumped into Carson Mason in the car supplies aisle and steeled myself. He and I had been in the same grade all through school and friendly, but he was Mr. Campbell's nephew.

"Carson."

"Josh," he nodded. "I can't believe there's nothing anyone can do to Hanson. He could've shot you. That's fucking unbelievable."

I let out the breath I'd been holding. "Thanks, Carson."

"He's getting his due, though. Don't worry about that. He's lost the contract for training the resort ranch horses."

"Really?"

"Yup. My brother-in-law's working there now. He told me. Said he thinks they're going to be giving you a call soon."

"That'd be nice. Thanks for the news, Carson."

"You bet. And if you ever want to go out, I'm hanging out at the Lonesome Whistle Bar now. Won't go near Cunningham's. Call me. We can meet up there."

"I'll do that, Carson."

At the grocery store, it was more of the same. The folks I saw that were my age still nodded at me. Most of my aunt's friends said hello to both of us, or at least to her. I guess that made us let down our guards. Then we ran into Velma Baker in the canned goods aisle.

"Velma!" my aunt called to her favorite cousin. Velma was about ten years older than my aunt, tall and thin, with long white hair piled high atop her head so she looked even taller and thinner, pinched almost.

"I'm so glad to see you," my aunt said. They had been close since they were young. "I was getting worried when I didn't hear from you these past couple of weeks. Have you been on a trip?"

"I have not," she said sharply. Then she pitched her voice loud enough so probably half the store could hear. "I can't talk to you as long as that sodomite is living at your ranch, Kate, and you know that very well. Why haven't you and Karl turned him out?"

"Velma, what are you talking about?"

"No one else will tell you this, Kate, but I'm family and it's my duty. That queer is going straight to hell, and you and Karl will too if you don't force him to change or leave your place." She looked straight at me, hatefulness oozing out of her like pus.

"My aunt and uncle don't have anything to do with it." How dare this woman go after my aunt.

"It's your parents' fault," Velma answered, sure as she could be. "But you can change—"

"You leave my parents out of it too."

I was vibrating with barely controlled anger now. "Come on, Aunt Kate. Let's go."

But my aunt had found her own voice.

"Velma," she said plenty loud and clear, "I'm truly sorry we won't be speaking again. I'll pray for you to change about this."

"Pray for me…." the woman sputtered, searching for what to say next. Guess her religious script didn't have a comeback for that.

"Come on, Josh," Aunt Kate said. "We've got things to do."

Aunt Kate gave the cart a shove and was halfway down the aisle before I caught up.

We headed for checkout after that and didn't say anything until we reached the truck.

"I'll drive," I said, taking the keys out of her hand. "I think you might be a little too riled up."

"You have no idea," she said as she climbed in. She turned toward the backseat and kept on talking while I loaded the grocery bags into it. "That woman has some nerve. She doesn't even follow the Gospel when it comes to her own family. Do you realize," she said as she turned around again so she could see me after I'd climbed into the driver's seat, "that her oldest son has been in prison for four years, and she has never visited him?"

"He's probably grateful."

At that, my aunt broke into a laugh that didn't stop until after I'd pulled out of the grocery parking lot and onto Highway 89.

"Oh Josh," she said between gasps for air. "If your sense of humor is that good, I can quit worrying. You are going to get through this just fine."

I still wasn't sure. But I was happy she was laughing.

TWENTY-FIVE

I'D JUST finished dinner when the knock came at my door. I figured it was Sarah. I'd heard her car pull up at Jesse's. She'd been at his place a couple of times since our talk, and I was glad about that, even though my brother still wasn't talking to me.

But it wasn't just Sarah. Jesse was behind her when I opened the door, and he had his hand on her shoulder, and they both looked anxious. I started worrying right away.

"What's the matter?"

Jesse cleared his throat. "Can we come in?"

I held the door open. Sarah came in first.

"Hey, Josh," she whispered as she hugged me, holding on a little longer than usual. Then she sat in my Gran's favorite leather easy chair.

Jesse followed behind her without looking at me. There was an alien restlessness about him as he sat on the arm of the same chair. His right leg pulsed up and down, his boot heel clicking loud on the hardwood floor.

I stayed standing behind the couch, keeping it and the table like a protective barrier between us.

"What's the matter?" Something was definitely wrong, but was it with my aunt or my uncle?

"Sit down, okay?" Jesse asked. He still wasn't looking at me, but Sarah had a quivery look on her face like someone had died.

I knew who it was. "What's happened to Dane?"

Sarah winced.

"Jesse, damn it, tell me right now. Where is he?"

My brother swiped his jaw with his hand and then rested it on Sarah's back.

"He's in Afghanistan."

"Not funny."

Jesse sighed and picked some imaginary fuzz off his knee.

"That phone call Dane mentioned the night he left? It was one of our former Ranger commanders. The guy has a private security company now, working all over the world. He called Dane about some high-level rescue job in Afghanistan, and Dane left."

"Rescuing who?"

"Josh, sit down."

"Rescuing who?" My voice was loud, and the room seemed small. "For how long? He didn't re-enlist, did he?"

Jesse got up and took a few steps around the room. "No, he didn't re-enlist. It's a private job. And he didn't tell me what it was specifically. If I had to guess, I'd say it's the five humanitarian aid workers the news reports say are missing from Kandahar, but I'm not sure."

"Why the hell isn't the Army rescuing them?"

"They're not Americans, according to the news."

"Why's anyone rescuing them?"

"Because al-Qaeda has them."

"How dangerous is it? When's he coming back?"

"I don't know."

"Don't you hide things from me. How'd you find out about this anyway? Did he call you?"

"He did, but he didn't say much. And I'm not trying to hide things from you, Josh. I'm telling you all I know. He went straight to Seattle, where the company's based. They made their plans there. He's been out of country for two days. He called me just before he left, and then to say he'd arrived. That's all, honest, Josh."

"Why the hell did he do that?"

"Please sit down, Josh."

I looked at Sarah. She was clasping and unclasping her hands. Jesse came up alongside me and tentatively took my arm. I let him steer me to the couch.

When I sat down, he sat next to me. He hunched over, his elbows on his knees, and stared at his clasped hands.

"I don't think it was the money—though he was offered a lot. He... I think it was because...." Jesse turned to me. "He was really sorry about things, Josh. I'm really sorry about things."

He looked at me at last, deep sorrow in his eyes.

"Oh, no. No. He couldn't be sorry and go back there. How could you let him do that? I can't believe you let him go."

"I think he needed to prove something to himself after what happened here," Jesse said slowly. "With his PTSD, and you and Hurricane. To show you he could save somebody, to prove to himself he's not damaged, not weak."

"I didn't think that." I was suddenly infuriated, at my brother, I guess, because I couldn't let myself be mad at Dane. "And you of all people should know that that PTSD shit doesn't matter to me."

"It matters to him, Josh. You've got to understand that about him. He's proud of his ability to handle any circumstances, and he hasn't managed that here. He cares about people who can't protect themselves, and he'll fight for them and for the people he cares about. It's how we measure our worth."

He looked up at Sarah, like he was making sure he had his words right.

"He doesn't care about me then... or he wouldn't have done this."

I started shaking. I was trying so hard to keep the anger and fear in, to keep Jesse from seeing.

"Josh, that's not true." He was quiet again before continuing. "I think he loves you."

His voice broke as he said it, and I looked into his face. He was staring at the floor, his lower lip quivering.

He looked up at Sarah again, and I followed his gaze. She gave him a tiny smile, her eyes shining with encouragement and love. I'd have liked to have someone look at me like that. Jesse nodded at her and turned to me again.

"Josh, I love you too, and I've made a bunch of mistakes." He rushed on to get all the words out. "Everything I've done since Hanson told everybody. I've done it all wrong. If I hadn't been so mad about your not telling me sooner... No, that's not right. It's not your fault, Josh, it's mine. It's mine. And I was wrong."

I saw deep shame in his eyes. "If I hadn't reacted how I did to your being gay, Dane might have felt he could tell you he cared about you, that he could tell me about himself. Shit, that he could stay. I am so sorry, Josh. When I realized Dane was gay, I knew I didn't care. He was still Dane, the Army buddy who saved my life, who was like a big brother to me."

He looked at me now like he was asking for something.

"And I realized I shouldn't care that my little brother was gay either." He swallowed hard and glanced at Sarah again before looking back down at his feet.

"Please forgive me, Josh."

I stared at him. I didn't know how to say what I felt. I touched his shoulder. When he looked at me again, I nodded. He nodded back, his lips in a tight line, his eyes blinking hard.

"What are his chances... of coming home?"

My brother glanced at the ceiling and around the room, then stared at his feet again.

"Tough," he said quietly. "They think the aid workers are hidden in Pakistan now, in a mountain valley that's hard to reach and harder to get out of."

"Oh, God." I was suddenly very, very cold.

I felt strong arms wrap around me as Jesse pulled me into his chest. Then Sarah was on my other side, holding me too, and rubbing my back.

"I know, little brother. I know."

They held me together like that for a long time, none of us talking. I managed not to cry, but I shook some. Finally, Sarah broke the stillness.

"Why don't you stay with us tonight?"

"Nah, I don't want to cramp you guys." I gave her a smile, small but real, and stood up. "I'll be okay, and I'll see you in the morning."

I looked at my brother. "Thanks for telling me, Jesse."

He nodded and stood up. "You sure you're okay?"

"Yeah." I walked them to the door. "Tomorrow," I promised as I let them out.

They walked arm in arm back to Jesse's, glancing back my way once. Then they went inside his house and shut the door.

I left all the lights in the living room on and went searching for where I'd finally hid Dane's jacket when I couldn't stand to look at it anymore. I put it on and slipped out my back door.

It was cold and dark. I pulled Dane's coat tighter around me and walked awhile through the back pasture.

Away from the lights of the house, I stopped and looked up. No moon. Just a billion stars and the edge of the Milky Way in the sky. I knew it was sometime close to noon in Afghanistan. There'd been a time when I always knew what time it was in Afghanistan and Iraq.

Where was Dane, and what was he doing? The memory of our last times together popped into my mind one after another fast, like popcorn in a too-hot popper. Dane fucking me so deep I felt he'd be there forever. Me calling him a coward as he walked away.

Now he might die. Would that horrible minute be his last memory of me? Pain that was nearly physical made me stumble. I hugged my stomach and dropped to my knees.

"Moron," I whispered to the sky. I wanted to scream, but I didn't want anyone to know how angry I was. I had to keep it inside. If it leaked out, it might hurt Dane.

"What were you thinking? You didn't have to prove anything to me." I rocked back and forth. "All you had to do was care. Why couldn't you care about me? Jesse is wrong. You don't love me. If you did, you wouldn't have done this. Oh God, Dane, please come back."

I knew I wouldn't get an answer, just like I knew he wouldn't come back here. But if he didn't return anywhere at all….

I stopped that thought, but it crept back again and again, leaving me colder each time it did. Something inside me went numb altogether. That was a good thing, I decided.

TWENTY-SIX

I WAS up early the next morning. Or maybe I never slept. I went to the corral to take care of Sugarpie and Hector and to walk Hurricane through his physical therapy routine.

Today, it was therapy for me too, moving slowly around the corral, paying attention to nothing but Hurricane's gait, breathing, and reactions.

"Hey, I thought you might like some coffee." Sarah stepped inside the corral with two thermos mugs.

I grabbed one as Hurricane and I went by. "Thanks."

"He's looking real good."

"He's going to have a big depression in his neck. But Hanson could have done a lot worse."

"I hear Mel Evans has left town," she said.

"No kidding."

"Yeah. A lot of people figure that means Hanson was behind everything, and they're kind of shunning him. He's lost some business."

I nodded. It was all the justice I would get, so I should have been pleased. Maybe I would have been yesterday. Today, it really didn't matter. I had said that before, when Hurricane was first shot. Now I really knew. What happened to Ray Hanson didn't matter. And I couldn't do a damn thing to affect what really did matter.

"What you thinking about?" Sarah called as Hurricane and I made another turn around the corral.

"When did Dane call Jesse?"

"Yesterday."

She pulled a peppermint out of her pocket. Hurricane sniffed the air, turned, and headed right for her and stopped, waiting. She held it out to him and rubbed his nose as he chomped it.

"I knew I could get you to stop," she said to him.

"When does he expect to hear from Dane again?"

Sarah frowned. "Dane didn't say when he'd call again. He doesn't. Jesse told you everything Dane told him, and everything he could figure out between the lines."

"But he knew Dane was leaving before Dane told me."

"He knew Dane had gotten that call—that's a fine distinction, Josh," Sarah said carefully. "I know because I asked Jesse these same questions, believe me. Jesse didn't know what Dane was going to do, and he did ask Dane to stay."

"But Dane didn't want to." I nudged Hurricane to start walking again.

It was as simple as that. Once I was outed, we were through. I should just accept he wasn't coming back, whether he survived the mission or not. God, it hurt to think that. I knew I'd never get the images of him and my feelings for him out of my mind.

Was Guy feeling as bad as I was? Is this what I'd done to him? Crap, I really deserved what was happening to me if that was so. But that didn't mean Dane deserved to be hurt or killed.

And Dane. Was he glad to be rid of me? Was being with me really so horrible that going back to Afghanistan was an improvement?

"Josh? Josh!"

I looked up. Sarah was walking toward me, her phone to her ear.

"Jesse says we're to head for the big house for lunch when you're through, and he wants to know when that might be."

I shrugged. "Another fifteen minutes."

"Okay, I'll tell him and wait for you."

Great. Lunch with everybody. I didn't want to. I didn't want to talk to anyone. But I couldn't do that to Jesse. He'd sincerely apologized yesterday, and I had to make sure he didn't doubt that I accepted it. And Uncle Karl and Aunt Kate. They were really standing by me, even though it was costing them. I should show them I was grateful.

Hurricane and I finished his therapy, and I turned him out to pasture. Jesse was standing by Sarah when I got back.

"Did you get any sleep?" he asked.

I shook my head.

"This is gonna be tough."

"Yeah."

The three of us headed for the big house, Jesse holding Sarah's hand. I wished I had someone to hold mine.

When we walked into the kitchen, Aunt Kate wrapped her arms around me. "We just have to believe he's going to come back to us, Josh," she said at last.

I nodded. Still, I didn't think that numb part inside me would allow me to believe that.

"Will you set the table?"

I did, but I was just going through the motions. Lunch was the same, and not just for me. A dark cloud seemed to hang over the whole table. No one talked until Jesse came up with a ridiculous plan for Sarah and me to help him check cattle.

"Isn't that what you have hired help for?"

"Gave them the day off," he told me.

"Sorry, I have to grade papers," Sarah said.

"Josh, you have to help me then."

So we climbed in his truck after we finished eating and headed for the pastures.

"God, I never realized until now what it was like for you guys, always worrying and waiting to hear from me when I was in the Rangers," he said. "It was a lot easier being over there."

"Yeah."

"I don't see how anybody stands it."

"Yeah."

He parked the truck and turned toward me. "Josh, I wish I could figure a way to make it up—"

"Jesse, it's okay. I understand, really. And I wish I hadn't been afraid to tell you that Sarah and I weren't ever going to get married. I could have done that."

"You don't need to be sorry. I'm the one who drew the conclusion. How could you know, really, what I wanted? We never talked about it, and I wasn't always sure myself."

"You're sure now?"

"I really am. I'll treat her right, Josh."

"I know you will."

He was still for a few minutes, thinking.

"Josh, it's okay for you to get mad at me. I won't disappear or die."

I huffed and pointed my finger at him. "See? I knew this was going to be a problem if you and Sarah got together. You'd talk about me."

"Hey, Sarah didn't say anything."

I glared at him, and he held up his hands in mock surrender. "All right, but only because I asked," he said. "And give me some credit. I half figured it out all on my own."

"That's crap, and you know it." I looked him straight in the eye. "Or else falling in love is making you sensitive. You'd better be worried about that."

He slugged me. I grinned and he did, too, and we got out of the truck and walked through the herd, reviewing each animal, pointing out details to each other, and stopping for a hands-on inspection now and then. This was the way things had been with us before. It was good to be doing this again.

After we climbed back in the truck, I got up the nerve to ask the question that had been on my mind since he'd told me about the phone call. "When do you think he'll call again?"

"He didn't say, but I think he will before they launch the mission."

I nodded. "When?"

Jesse shook his head. "That's the hard one. Weather is getting iffy there. They're headed into winter, same as us. They'll want a dark night. It's a couple weeks before there's no moon again. But it's not clear they've got the best intel yet, or that they feel comfortable with the plan or their practice runs."

He started up the truck.

"Do you want to go out tonight, Josh? Maybe we take Sarah dancing to forget for a while?"

I thought a bit before answering. "I don't think so. I know you'll think I'm a coward, but I don't know if I'll ever be up for going to Cunningham's again."

"I don't think you're a coward. Not at all, Josh. I mean that. And I didn't mean Cunningham's. I haven't been back since that night. Won't go until or unless you go. Sarah and I agree on that."

"You don't have to on account of me."

Jesse put his hand on my shoulder. "We want to do that for you, Josh. We are both one hundred percent behind you."

"Thanks."

Checking the cattle killed a couple of hours. Then Jesse went off to check on some equipment, and I headed for the big barn. I lost myself there for a few hours, checking on animals, tack, and feed supplies.

We all had dinner together, and Jesse, Sarah, and I did cleanup. A long, restless night loomed for us all. We joined Aunt Kate and Uncle Karl in the family room. They each sat in their favorite recliner chair. He was watching TV, and she was knitting.

Sarah and Jesse sat down on the couch, and I took a spot on the floor, leaning against an ottoman.

"With all of you here, I want to bring up an idea I have for next summer," Aunt Kate said, looking up from her knitting. It was some big blue thing, probably a prayer shawl for church. She was always knitting them. I didn't understand how praying and big knit blankets went together, but she claimed they helped people. Then again, if she could tell me one would help bring Dane back to me, I knew I wouldn't hesitate to wear one all day every day.

Uncle Karl hit the mute button on the remote and turned toward her, an amused look on his face. "An idea for next summer?" he repeated. "Do tell, Kate."

"Brace yourself," my brother whispered to Sarah.

Aunt Kate shot him the killer look. Then she smiled and put down her knitting needles.

"I've been reading a lot on PFLAG…."

"Parents, Families, and Friends of Lesbians and Gays," Sarah supplied for Jesse.

He glared at me. "Thanks a lot," he mouthed. But he was smiling.

This was so like my aunt. Gay pride was going to be her new crusade because one of us was affected. Heck, she was still big into sending letters and packages to soldiers overseas. She had been since Jesse's first deployment. Why hadn't I realized long ago that she would react this way?

I thought back on Sarah's challenge to give my family more credit and glanced at her. She smiled at me like she had read my mind.

"Now then," Aunt Kate continued, "I think we should set aside one week next summer that's only for gay teens and their families."

"Hmmm," Uncle Karl said.

"That's a great idea," Sarah said.

"Just make sure you put up condom dispensers by the swim pond, because they'll all be having sex every night," Jesse said.

Sarah and Aunt Kate shrieked his name in unison. Uncle Karl frowned.

"What?" Jesse said. "I don't care if they're straight or gay, the one thing all teenage boys want to do is—"

"That's enough, Jesse," Sarah scolded.

"Why don't you two just get married right now and get it over with?" I asked. "You already sound like an old married couple."

"That is not what I had in mind," Aunt Kate said to Jesse.

"You don't want Sarah and me to get married?" he asked.

"That's not what I meant either," my aunt sputtered.

Sarah blushed. Jesse started laughing, and Uncle Karl joined in. My aunt was reacting just the way Jesse wanted her to, the way only he could make her. I began to laugh too, and it felt... good.

"Why do you want to do this, Kate?" my uncle asked at last.

"There are awful stories out there about the bullying of gay children," she replied. "Look what happened to Josh."

"Hey, I'm not a child."

"Oh, I don't know," Jesse said. "You couldn't defend yourself very well from what I heard."

"It was four on one, and the first guy I punched fell at my feet and I tripped over him." I sat up straight ready to take on my brother.

"That's how you're going to tell it," Jesse said, his dimples deepening as he grinned.

"I am." The look on his face made me start laughing again.

"Anyway," my aunt interrupted. She sounded irritated, but it was an act. "I think it would be great to bring kids from all over the country together here to ride, fish, tour the park, and talk with each other. Maybe we bring in some special counselor for that week. Summer camps for gay children are all over the Internet."

"What week would we pick and how would we get the word out?" Uncle Karl asked.

"We could look at the week this summer that had the fewest repeat families and choose that one," she answered. "We don't want to disrupt too many of our regulars."

"I could help with finding the counselor," Sarah said.

"I suppose we'd just advertise on different Internet sites, or in a special magazine," Jesse said.

"And if we weren't full up that week, well, it wouldn't hurt us for just one week, Karl," Aunt Kate said.

"You do realize some of your friends and neighbors are going to react badly to this?" Velma Baker's face sprang to my mind.

"Bring it," Jesse said fiercely.

"What about the hands?"

"We'd be honest with the full-timers and the summer help too, and if they didn't like it, they could find work elsewhere. Simple," Jesse replied.

Sarah smiled broadly at me.

"Besides those concerns," Uncle Karl said, "how do you feel about the idea, Josh?"

"I like it."

"Then we'll do it," he said, looking around the room. "We need to get the publicity and the full season calendar out in the next two weeks to meet our Thanksgiving deadline, though," he added.

"Not a problem, dear," my aunt replied. "I've been working on that already."

"I'll bet you have," he said, smiling at her.

He hit the sound button on the remote again.

TWENTY-SEVEN

SUNDAY afternoon, Sarah went back to her apartment to get ready for school, and Jesse talked me into coming over to his house. We sat in front of the TV for a while watching the football game, but not really watching it either.

"Josh? Would you move in with me while we...."

"Yeah." My reply was immediate, my gut reaction. Neither of us wanted to wait alone. "I'll move my clothes later."

"Great! Let's go into Livingston and get groceries then."

"You just want a cook."

"That's not all."

"I know."

We returned with enough groceries for an army. We should have made a list. I made pizza for dinner, and we sat around and watched the night game.

"I'll get your old bed ready for you," Jesse offered.

"I'm good on the couch. I've got it all warmed up."

He nodded and disappeared. A few minutes later, he returned with a pillow and blankets.

"You going to tuck me in too?"

He smiled sheepishly. "If you want. Lift your head."

He put the pillow under my head and draped the blankets around me.

"The hands and I will take care of the horses by the big barn tomorrow. You concentrate on Hurricane and stuff over here, okay?"

"You sure?"

"Yeah. You need to take it easy. You look like you're not getting any sleep."

He was worried about me, on top of his own worries for Dane.

"Jesse, you don't have to make anything up to me. We're back to being like always on my end."

"I know, but maybe I want to… be extra nice to you."

"Hey, I won't argue with that."

"Night, little brother."

"Night, Jesse."

I ENDED up staying at Jesse's for the next couple weeks, and they seemed like they dragged on longer than the whole rest of my life had lasted. Jesse and I went our separate ways sometimes, and sometimes I joined him to help out with the cattle. Sarah stopped by each afternoon, and we all ate dinner with Aunt Kate and Uncle Karl. Sometimes she spent the night at Jesse's too, and I stayed on the couch and put a pillow over my head. But they were careful to be real quiet. I never heard anything.

The nights were the worst. When Jesse and I were alone, we passed the time watching news reports on Afghanistan or sports programs, or staring at the phone.

Finally one night, the thing rang.

Jesse jumped out of his chair to answer it, and I hit the mute on the TV. Suddenly, there was nothing in the room but Jesse and the telephone. I barely breathed as I listened to him talk.

"Dane, buddy, it's good to hear from you."

Jesse shot me an excited look, and then he didn't talk for a bit. Clearly Dane was talking about something important. I started pacing the room.

"Oh, yeah, I understand," he said at last. "Hey, man, you're not going to believe—Josh is here. You want to talk to him?"

I took a couple quick steps toward Jesse, then realized he was frowning. Another silence that stretched too long followed.

"I understand."

Jesse looked at me but kept the phone plastered to his ear.

Then his lips started moving, though no sound came out. "Say something to him," he mouthed.

I gulped. Jesse held the phone away from his ear.

"Tell him…," I began.

Jesse waved his hand to get my attention. "Louder," he whispered.

My fists clenched. I cleared my throat and started again, louder this time, picturing Dane's face in front of me. "Tell Dane that we all want the ranch to be his home always, no matter what… Tell him I'm waiting for him—if he wants. Ask him, ask him if that's worth the coming home."

Jesse nodded at me and started talking into the phone again. "Yeah, bro. Got it. Do the job and get back here…."

"Dane!" I shouted. "Stay alert, Dane!"

And then I couldn't breathe. I couldn't bear to hear another thing without hearing Dane's voice too. I bolted out the door, and it banged shut behind me. I didn't remember pushing it hard, but I must have.

On the front porch, I wasn't sure what to do. I had no place to go really. I leaned against the railing and stared up at the stars, clutching my arms to my sides against the cold.

After a while, I heard Jesse open the door. When I turned around, he was holding it open.

"Come on back in, Josh."

"Why wouldn't he talk to me? What's wrong?"

"Nothing's wrong."

"Is he on his way home?"

"No. They're launching the mission within twenty-four hours. He wanted us to know."

"You to know. He wanted you to know. Why wouldn't he talk to me?"

Jesse rubbed his forehead like he was trying to scrape paint off it.

"He wanted to let you know too. But he needs to keep his mind on the job. Josh, Dane is leading the team, and he can only think about the job right now. That's why he didn't want to talk to you. The only reason. You understand me?"

I stared at him like he was talking in a foreign language.

"I mean it, Josh. He heard you. You said just the right things. He was glad to hear you."

"You don't know that. He didn't say that."

"I know it's true. It's what I'd want to hear if I was in his place."

He opened the door wider. "Will you come in now? It's freezing out here."

Jesse wouldn't move until I did, so I made myself go inside. He shut the door behind me.

Back in the living room, he pointed me toward the sofa, and I sat down. He walked over to lean against the stone wall behind the wood stove. I couldn't tell if he really needed to lean against it to support himself after the phone call or if he was simply warming up.

"When will it be over, Jesse?"

"He couldn't say things straight out, you understand? But this is a crazy-tough mission. It could take hours. It could take days. They have to get in position and then wait for things to fall into place."

"And if things don't?"

"Then they force them. At some point, you just gotta make a move. And that's all up to the leader, to Dane, to decide. But he's part of a great team of guys. I know one of them. He was with us in the Rangers. He was really, really good at a lot of things."

"What are their chances?"

He looked at me like he wished I hadn't asked. He stepped away from the wall and bent over, rubbing both palms on his jeans for a bit before he looked at me and answered. "They're not the best. But Dane is, and so are the guys with him. And they all want to come home. Especially Dane. You made sure he's feeling that way. You just keep remembering that, you understand?" Jesse's last remark came out louder and fiercer than the rest, like a kind of command of his own.

I nodded, staring at him, trying to read between the lines. Despite his reassurances, I was pretty certain that if I imagined the worst possible things, I was closest to the truth.

He walked into the kitchen. I heard the refrigerator door open and close. He returned with two bottles of beer. He handed me one and raised his.

"To Dane and the mission."

"To Dane and the mission." I tapped his bottle and downed half of mine.

Jesse sat down on the couch next to me, and we looked at the stove awhile. Every now and then we'd hear a hiss or crackle. Eventually, he got up to add more wood, and I finally remembered to turn the TV sound back on.

THE phone didn't ring the next day or the next night, or the night after that. I went through the motions and did what I had to during the day. I even went to bed at night, but I never slept. I kept remembering that first time with Dane, when I discovered all his scars.

The second night, even though I tried not to, I pictured him getting new ones. I couldn't stop myself, hard as I tried. It was like a real-life horror movie taking place before my eyes, full of violent, bloody red images of Dane being stabbed, shot, blown up, tortured. I got up and started pacing around the house.

When it was clear I'd woken Jesse, I went outside and walked around the house till my fingers froze. I came back in finally, and wrapped myself in Dane's jacket. I'd brought it to my brother's house along with my clothes. It still smelled like him, and it was the only thing that helped. I didn't sleep, but at least I could sit still when I wrapped myself in it.

"Come back, Dane. Please come back." I chanted it like a prayer until the sun came up.

THE fourth afternoon, Jesse came looking for me while I was exercising Hurricane. The horse was the only thing keeping me together. I spent most of every day with him.

"How you holding up?"

"Not. How about you?"

"Not good, but better than you. Sarah thinks the three of us should go out to dinner."

"But what if someone calls?"

"Whoever it is will leave a message. They've got my cell. Dane promised me that we'd be contacted by the company, whatever…."

He didn't finish the sentence, and I didn't want him to. "Where you want to go?"

"You pick," he said.

"Cunningham's."

Jesse looked at me in surprise.

"Why not? So many things could go wrong that it's sure to keep my mind off Dane."

"Works for me," he said. "And don't worry, Josh. I've got your back."

"I know."

"I'll buy."

"You bet you will."

Sarah agreed to meet us at the bar, and we took off. Jesse pulled into the parking lot, turned off the truck, and opened his door. But I hesitated. He put his hand on my shoulder.

"It's going to be okay, Josh. I'm backing you. And if some dumb fucker wants to fight, we'll fight and we'll win."

I nodded. "I appreciate that. Let's not let it go that far, though."

"Okay."

We walked in, and I scanned the room only long enough to locate Sarah, who was holding down a table for six. I headed straight for it without looking anywhere else. Jesse followed behind me.

"Awful big table," I said to her. "You expecting company?"

"You just never know," she said, a big smile on her face. It seemed like she was hiding something, but I couldn't figure what.

"Okay," I said at last. I sat down beside her.

"How are you doing?"

I shrugged.

"So, two PBRs and a Coors?" Jesse asked.

"I'll just have an iced tea," Sarah said.

"Coming up." He headed for the bar.

"What do you suppose Billy Cunningham is going to say to him?"

"If he's smart, he'll say, 'Coming right up,'" Sarah replied. "I don't think he wants to lose the Brooks business forever. And from what I hear, several regulars have stayed away since you got thrown out."

"You're kidding?"

"No, I'm not. They don't like the idea of patronizing a place that discriminates—unless it's against stupidity and meanness."

I thought back to what Carson Mason had said in the grocery store, and it was like I felt the tiniest spark of warmth strike that numb spot inside me.

Jesse returned with the drinks and set them down, but he didn't sit down.

"Looks like I need to go back to the bar," he said, glancing over my shoulder.

I turned around to find my aunt and uncle behind me. I smiled then, for the first time since Dane's phone call.

"Mind if we join you?" Aunt Kate asked.

"Not at all," Sarah said, trying to sound like she was surprised. I knew she'd organized it. I should have known when I spotted the size of the table.

"I'll have what Sarah's having," Aunt Kate said, slipping in beside me. She leaned over and kissed my cheek.

"And I'll have a beer." Uncle Karl sat down, and Jesse turned to head back to the bar.

But Billy Cunningham was coming toward our table. I stiffened. Jesse took a step back toward us, and Uncle Karl stood up. Aunt Kate and Sarah drew closer to me like mother birds shielding a chick.

Billy saw it too, and a nervousness settled on his face. He stopped a few feet away from the table and cleared his throat.

"Good evening, everybody," he said, nodding at Jesse, Uncle Karl, and me. "I'm really pleased to have you back, especially you, Josh."

I nodded. My aunt and uncle relaxed.

"Good to see you," my uncle said amiably.

Billy eased a bit at that. "The special is a shredded beef sandwich with mashed potatoes and gravy," he said. "And your drinks are on the house."

"That's really nice of you, Billy," Aunt Kate said sweetly.

"More than hamburgers tonight, then?" Jesse asked.

Billy smiled at last. "Yeah, I got a new cook. Probably not as good as you, Josh," he looked at me expectantly.

He was really trying, I could tell. I nodded. "I'm glad for you, Billy. I'm sure things are going easier because of it."

"They are," he said. He swallowed and fiddled with the towel that was draped over his shoulder. "I'm sorry, Josh. No excuses. There aren't any. I'm just real sorry."

"Thanks, Billy. I appreciate that." I stood up and shook his hand, and he gripped mine even as the rest of him really relaxed. I nodded at him again and saw the gratitude in his eyes, and I realized in that instant how really good you can feel when you forgive someone.

Everything else moved along like normal. Uncle Karl repeated his and Aunt Kate's drink order, and we all asked for the special.

"Coming up," Billy said and headed back to the bar. Jesse and Uncle Karl sat down.

"He's not a bad boy," Aunt Kate said to me after he'd left.

I hadn't thought of Billy Cunningham or myself as a boy in a lot of years, but I knew what she was trying to say. "Hanson took us both by surprise, I think."

"I'm proud of you, Josh."

"Why, Uncle Karl?"

"You didn't have to be so agreeable. Anybody would have understood if you hadn't accepted his apology."

"I had to meet him halfway."

"You went more than half. That's why I'm proud."

We made small talk after that, and I focused on not looking around the bar. Jesse was doing enough of that for both of us.

Once, I caught him doing it, and he smiled at me. "Just keeping my word, Josh."

I nodded. The sandwiches came. They were really good.

"I wonder who this cook is?" Sarah said.

"We're going to have to ask," Aunt Kate replied. "I really like the seasonings in this gravy. I want the recipe."

I laughed, and she smiled. And then I heard Ray Hanson's voice coming across the bar.

"Don't you know faggots aren't welcome in Montana, Brooks?" Again he was loud enough that half the place could hear him.

"Maybe we should help him out, boss," one of his goons said. I recognized the man I'd tripped over in the fight.

Jesse and Uncle Karl rose in unison. The hair on the back of my neck stood up as I got to my feet. I still couldn't bring myself to look around the bar, but I didn't really have to. I knew everyone was looking at us.

When Sarah moved to stand up with us, Jesse put a hand on her shoulder.

"Sarah, Aunt Kate," he said, never moving his eyes off Hanson and his two hands as they advanced toward us. "Please move yourselves and your chairs behind Josh so Uncle Karl and I can stand next to him."

They both did what he said without arguing.

"You need help leaving this bar, faggot?" Hanson asked as he stopped a few feet from the table. "Because we'd like nothing better than to help you outta here like we done before."

"The word is 'gay,' Hanson," my uncle said. "And my nephew doesn't need any help because he's not leaving. You might want to think about it, though."

Hanson stared at my uncle without replying.

"Look," Uncle Karl continued, his voice low so only Hanson would hear, "we all know your real beef has always been that Josh is a better horse trainer."

"That faggot can't best me at nothing, old man," Hanson said, his voice even louder.

"Oh, he's better than you at everything," Uncle Karl replied, raising his voice at last. "Everybody in this bar knows what kind of man you are, Ray. Now why don't you just leave real quietly and let everybody go back to having a good time?"

Hanson's face turned red. "I don't take orders from an old man."

"You'll take them from me, Hanson." Billy Cunningham had emerged from the kitchen and was striding toward our table.

"I was wrong the last time you and Josh met here," he said as he stopped about five feet off to Hanson's right. "I should have tossed just you out then, not Josh. I'm doing the right thing this time. And if you don't want to leave by yourself now, the sheriff will be here in a few minutes to help you out."

Jesse spoke quietly. "You can't win, Hanson. Why don't you walk out on your own and save yourself the humiliation."

Hanson glanced at each of us, his hands clenching and unclenching at his sides, and then he looked around the bar. No one was coming to his defense. In fact, the men at the three tables immediately around ours had risen and taken a few steps toward Uncle Karl.

I thought I saw sweat break out on Hanson's face. He glanced at his two hired hands, who were really only good at fighting if they got the jump on a man. A look like fear crossed his face before he raised his chin.

"We don't want to stay in a bar that serves 'gays,' Cunningham," he sneered. "Anybody who doesn't like drinking with queers is welcome to leave with us."

He turned around, and his men followed him out the door. Nobody else did.

"Well, now, that was something I didn't think I'd be doing again at my age, boys," Uncle Karl said to no one in particular. Then he helped Aunt Kate move back to the table. "I think I'm ready for another beer."

A chuckle went round the room, and the men behind Uncle Karl returned to their seats. Jesse helped Sarah sit down again at the table.

"I'm really sorry about that," Billy said. "I didn't see him come in, or this wouldn't have happened. He's not welcome here anymore."

"Thanks, Billy."

"Thank you, Josh, for giving me another chance."

I nodded, and Billy grinned and went off to get Uncle Karl's beer.

Sarah turned to Jesse and then to Uncle Karl and me. "You guys sure know how to show a girl a good time."

When we left the bar later, several folks stood up to talk to Uncle Karl or Jesse or me, and to shake my hand. Turned out I got a better surprise than I was expecting at Cunningham's.

TWENTY-EIGHT

SEVEN long days later, again in the evening, the second phone call came.

Jesse answered, and I could tell right away it wasn't Dane. I went numb.

Jesse waved his hand wildly to get my attention. "He's alive," he mouthed. Then he listened and repeated "Uh-huh" so many times, I thought I'd lose my mind before he hung up.

"What?"

"They're back. With all the aid workers too. It wasn't easy. One of their translators was working for al-Qaeda, but Dane caught on early. He hadn't let on that he understood Pashto too. One of his team members didn't make it. It'll be on the news in the next few hours."

"What about Dane?" My voice shook, and the hairs on the back of my neck stood up. I was sure Jesse was leaving out something important.

"He killed the guy, but he was stabbed three times."

I must have turned white, because Jesse rushed over and forced me to sit down. He even tried to push my head toward my knees.

"Don't worry, Josh. He's not gonna die—"

I popped my head up fast. "You're sure?"

"He won't," Jesse repeated. "But he's left the hospital in Okinawa against doctor's orders, and they don't know where he is."

"They don't know where he is? They've got an injured American wandering around on an island full of Japanese, and they can't find him?" I was furious.

"Calm down, Josh. Really. He's okay and he can take care of himself. Remember that. The security company thinks he's gotten himself on a commercial flight and he's headed this way."

Jesse paused and looked me in the eye. "He named you as his next of kin, Josh, on his paperwork. I think he's headed here too."

Me, his next of kin? The news barely registered. It sure wasn't enough to make me happy, or even calm. Where the hell was he?

"When will he get here?"

"I don't know. If he's smart, he won't drive many hours a day. But if he was smart, he would have stayed in the hospital longer. Damn idiot. And we have that big snowstorm coming in. That'll slow him down." Jesse wiped his face in exasperation. "It could be days before he gets here, Josh."

"Maybe he'll call?"

"Let's hope." But he didn't sound confident either.

BY LATE afternoon two days later, the storm was seriously blowing in. Jesse, Uncle Karl, and I had spent hours securing things around the ranch and our houses. We'd brought the horses and cattle into protected meadows and fed them over-well. It was freezing cold, and the wind howled and blew nonstop, sending the snow sideways. By nightfall, it was going to be impossible to see.

School let out early, and Sarah came straight to the ranch. Once my brother and I knew Uncle Karl and Aunt Kate were set at the big house, we joined her at Jesse's around sunset.

And still Dane didn't call. I was going crazy. All day I'd worried. Would he get here before the storm? What if he got stuck? Could he hole up somewhere and stay safe with the injuries he had? Was he coming here at all? And if he wasn't, where the hell was he? I wanted to kill him myself, I was so mad at him.

The three of us had just sat down to supper when a light knock sounded. I thought it was the wind. But Jesse flew out of his chair and headed for the front door. Sarah grabbed my hand.

I sat still listening for any noise from the living room, but all I heard was the kitchen clock ticking. I watched the second hand sweep along the face. The wind rattled the kitchen window, and I shivered with it.

Was Jesse moving in slow motion or what? I heard the front door open and shut, then Jesse talked to someone, but not loud enough that I could make out the words. Had one of the hands come by?

I waited some more, my free hand gripping my knee under the table, my mouth dry. What should I say if it was Dane? I'd been thinking up lines for two days, but I couldn't remember any of them now.

And what if it wasn't him?

"Come on in and eat." Jesse's words floated into the kitchen.

Then Dane was there, hunched in the doorway, letting the woodwork hold him up, with Jesse right behind him.

I glanced at him and looked away as quickly, afraid to meet his eyes in case I'd see something I couldn't bear. What I saw was enough. He looked worn-out and smaller.

I freed my hand from Sarah's and pushed up from the table. I still couldn't look in his face, or figure out if I wanted to apologize for calling him a coward or yell at him for scaring me like he had. I went to the cupboard and got him a plate and a glass and silverware.

"What do you want to drink?" I had meant to sound conversational, but my words came out angry and demanding.

"Hey to you too, cowboy. You look good."

"You look like shit." The words banged off the kitchen walls and rang in my ears. I made myself lower my voice. "Sit down and eat, and then you're going to bed."

I wanted to be kind to him. I really wanted to hug him. But my fear was leaking out all over the place. Suddenly I was yelling.

"Fuck al-Qaeda. I feel like killing you myself. What were you thinking going back there? And what did you think you were doing leaving that damn hospital early and then driving through a snowstorm?"

Sarah sat stunned and silent. Even Jesse didn't say anything.

Dane cocked his head and studied me, his face revealing nothing. I decided he hadn't given a lot of thought to how we'd left things. He hadn't wondered what I was thinking, what I was afraid of, the whole time he was gone. I could feel my anger climbing up my throat, burning like bile, choking me, as I stared right back at him.

Sarah broke the silence at last. "What Josh means, Dane, is we're all so glad you're back." She jumped out of her chair and headed for the living room. "I've got to call Kate and Karl right away and tell them."

She touched his cheek as she moved around him in the doorway, and he smiled at her. At her, not me.

She disappeared into the living room, and Jesse came into the kitchen finally. He went straight for the table and pulled out a chair. Dane sat down in it. Then Jesse sat down. He had a stupid big grin on his face.

I put the plate and silverware in front of Dane. He wore the tiniest hint of a grin too. If he was laughing at me, I was going to hurt him.

"So, you've learned to swear in the short time I've been gone?"

"Shut up."

I grabbed the plastic milk jug and filled his glass. But I had to pour slowly. My hands shook. I took a deep breath, watched them still, and put the glass down in front of Dane. That's when I saw the three big blotches, dull, dried red, on the back of his shirt. My stomach flipped, and my voice lost its edge.

"Dane, your back."

Jesse didn't say anything. So he'd seen them. But why wasn't he doing something?

Dane just shifted in his chair to look up at me. "Shh, cowboy. They stopped bleeding a couple hours after I left the hospital, and they don't hurt much. Sit down and let's eat. I've been hoping it would be stew night for two days now. You made it today, right?"

He passed his plate to Jesse. "Not too heavy to start," he instructed.

Jesse filled the plate and started making a plan.

"That's right, Dane. We'll eat and get you settled in for the night, then see tomorrow what's up with the storm." He picked up speed as he talked.

"You and Josh can sleep upstairs—"

"No." My voice was like a whip crack, too loud and too sharp. The two of them looked at me with surprise, and I felt my face redden. But I had things I needed to say to Dane. Things I needed to hear him say, and they weren't anything about the rescue mission and the conversation Jesse would start. "Dane and I are going home."

Jesse looked from me to Dane, who was smiling a big, satisfied smile now. I sat down.

"Okay," Jesse said, starting to spin in a new direction. "That's a good idea, Josh. You guys go back to the cabin. We'll see how things are in the morning. That's a plan."

Sarah practically skipped back into the room. "Karl and Kate are thrilled you're back safe, Dane. They hope they can see you tomorrow, and we can all celebrate together."

After that, nobody talked much through the meal except to ask for something to be passed. Once, Sarah asked Dane how he felt, and he said something about having had worse injuries. But I noticed he sat through the whole meal with his body hunched forward over the table. He never once leaned back in his chair.

I barely ate, my mind chewing through one thought after another. What if Dane didn't want to spend the night at my cabin after we ate? What if his going there was really only about kicking me good-bye, and he was here to stay with Jesse while he healed up?

Fifteen minutes later, Sarah kissed Dane and me good night. Jesse handed me his first aid kit and walked us out to Dane's truck. We all bent over against the wind, snow crystals flying at us. They felt like little knives slicing my face.

Dane got in on the passenger side. I hopped into the driver's seat. The truck felt cold as the grave. He leaned forward, bracing his arms on the dash, never touching his back to the seat. But he seemed to have more energy now that he'd eaten.

"We'll be there in a minute, and we'll get you in a hot shower," I said, revving the engine.

"I'm good, cowboy. Really, I'm good."

I hit the gas and the truck lurched forward, swerved, and gained traction. I couldn't see much, but I didn't need to. We covered the distance quickly.

I parked alongside the porch and walked Dane right into the bedroom, sat him on the edge of the bed along with the first aid kit, and headed into the bathroom to get the shower going. He didn't say a word.

When I returned, he hadn't moved. I wanted to tell him how glad I was to see him. But I was too afraid he wasn't moving because he was going to push me away once and for all now. I couldn't let it come to that.

I knelt down and went to work getting his boots and socks off. This close, I could smell him. Stale hospital and perspiration. I could make that go away. But what about what had happened between us? What had happened to him? He'd lost a member of his team. How would he handle that? What would he say? I felt like a rodeo bull waiting for a chute to spring me into an unknown arena.

Dane settled his hand on my head and moved it lightly through my hair, fluffing it up and smoothing it back down. Even when I finished with his boots, he kept doing it. It felt good and I didn't move to get up.

"I was so scared I wouldn't make it back here," he whispered. "Or if I did, that you'd be here with Guy or someone else."

"Shhh." I closed my eyes and lifted my face into his hand, rubbing my cheek against the calluses on his palm. His fingers were shaking.

"Cowboy, I was so stupid."

"No. Don't you ever say that to me. To anyone."

I regretted my words immediately. They were too intense. I was blowing this. Dane was still as cattle during the hottest part of the sweatiest day of summer, like he was backing up and reconsidering everything.

"I think you're going to have to help me," he whispered at last.

"Yeah." I stood and took off his shirt slowly so as not to hurt him. The bandages wrapped all around his torso front and back. They'd slipped some, revealing angry red-puffed skin around way too many stitches. And I was seeing just the smallest part of his injuries. I choked on a breath.

"They're all knife wounds, and they're stitched," he said matter-of-factly, heaving himself up from the bed. "They haven't bled again since that first day. I think the bandages will come off on their own in the shower."

He headed for the bathroom, and I followed. It was steamy in there now. Dane began removing his pants, and I concentrated on getting my own clothes off. When I looked up, he was naked and hard and watching me like a starved man.

Could he still want me? My face got hot. My eyes didn't leave his cock even as I moved to gently push him toward the shower and followed him in.

He ducked his head under the spray but kept his back away from the water and from me, like he didn't want me to see it. I lathered up his hair first. He made a little humming sound that told me he liked it, so I rubbed his head a long time with my fingertips before guiding him back under the water, being careful to keep the soap out of his eyes and off his back.

I turned his back toward me at last, soaped up a washcloth and started in on his arms and shoulders. I gave his butt a cursory swipe and moved down one leg and up the other. Next, I moved him away from the water and went to work unwrapping the bandages. He held his arms up out of the way. He didn't make a sound or a grimace, though I must have hurt him at least once. With the washcloth, I dribbled warm, soapy water over the scary number of stitches but didn't touch them directly.

I made myself quit counting them and watched pink swirls disappear down the shower drain instead.

The wounds looked to be deep, and one was much longer than the others. They looked like they were healing okay. All of them were on his right side, like someone had surprised him when his back was turned. I remembered he'd killed the traitor who'd done this to him, and I was glad.

Then I couldn't help myself. I bent my head and started to kiss the skin along the stitches. Light and feathery, nothing that would hurt, I kissed beside each cut. I wanted to make the wounds and the pain go away, to maybe make us both forget what I'd said before he left.

When his back trembled beneath my lips, I stopped. He turned to face me, his eyes clenched shut and water running down his cheeks. I couldn't tell if it was tears. They couldn't be tears. I raised a hand and smoothed them away with my thumb, and he kissed it.

"You were right," he whispered, not looking into my face. "I was a coward."

"That's not true." The words were out of my mouth as soon as he'd finished. "I was wrong. I was angry and stupid. I don't want to talk about that. Ever."

In that moment I knew I didn't care if I never heard his explanation for why he left. I didn't want to hear anyone ever say bad things about him, especially not Dane himself.

"Yes," he insisted. "I'm going to say this, Josh, or we've got nowhere to go."

Maybe it was being washed clean that made him have to say it. Maybe it was hearing him call me by my name that made me have to listen.

I gripped his hand and brought it to my cheek and held it there, staring all the while at his chest. "Okay."

His voice was no louder than the whisper of the water all around us.

"I ran," he choked out, "because I was too afraid to face what you had to face. I'd lied for so long about who I was. I couldn't face how other people would react, how your brother and your family would react.

"Within the first hour after I left, I knew I was wrong, that I was being a coward."

"*No!*"

He gripped my jaw and raised my head slightly, so I was looking at his neck. I watched his Adam's apple move as he swallowed hard and spoke again. "Yes. I was. But it was too late. I'd already committed to the mission, to the team. I wanted to call you so many times, to hear how things were with you, to tell you how much I admired how brave you were. I wanted to talk to you that night before the mission—"

"I understand. Jesse explained." I shook free of his hand and looked up into his face finally, searching his eyes so I could see when he understood all that was in mine. "It's all okay now. It's all okay forever. Nothing has changed about my love for you, except I love you more."

He started to shake, and I gripped his waist and pulled him close to me. We held each other until he stilled, until I began to worry that the hot water would turn to cold soon.

I took up the washcloth again and soaped it up, rubbing it in sudsy circles across his chest, slowly making my way lower. He stood still, his hands fisted at his side, his eyes clenched shut.

I'm just washing him, I told myself. But I brushed his cock, and it jumped.

He didn't move or open his eyes, so I dropped my slick hands down to his hips and massaged my way to his bellybutton with little circular motions. His hands relaxed. Still, he didn't open his eyes.

I cupped his balls with one hand and wrapped the other around his cock, sliding my fingers slowly up and down. He was dark against the white suds, hard and smooth. His balls clenched when I feathered my fingers over the pebbly skin.

He moved then, spreading his legs wider, and he put his hands on my shoulders. I thought he was just steadying himself, but the pressure increased. I looked up into his eyes, open now, intense and demanding as they swept from my face to my knees.

Yeah, I wanted it like this, to let him have all the control he wanted, forever if he wanted, as long as he wanted me. I went to my knees. I let the water rinse him off, then swallowed him in a gulp. I eased back and went to work with my tongue, teasing and licking him up and down.

A groan exploded out of him, like he'd been holding it and too many other things in way too long. He took my head gently in both his hands and pushed himself deep in my throat.

"Like that, cowboy. But put your hands behind your back." He stopped, then added, "Please."

I clasped my hands against the small of my back and let his hands hold me in place. He pumped in and out, and I swirled my tongue around his crown and slit.

He came fast, in an explosion, and I gulped hard and sucked him down. His hands stayed on my head like he didn't want to let me go. At last, he slumped a shoulder against the tile wall, his hands slipping to my shoulders.

I pushed myself up off the floor and reached out to gather him in my arms. He came into them with a hesitant shudder and gripped my waist. I thought maybe he was getting cold.

"Come on. Let's get out before the water goes cold."

But he leaned into me without moving, then gripped me tighter, burying his head in my neck.

"I didn't think you could ever want me again...." The pain behind his words was too much to hear.

"Let's get you to bed."

I guided him out of the shower and turned off the water. All the ideas I had about what else needed to be said turned off too. I didn't need him to tell me he loved me or anything else. Whatever was going to be between us was going to prove itself in the way we treated each other. And I knew how I wanted to treat him.

Without letting him go, I grabbed a towel and started lightly rubbing his head and arms. I patted his back, barely touching it, then took a step back and wrapped the towel around his waist. He still hadn't released me fully. I put a hand over one of his, teased his fingers into mine, and led him into the bedroom.

When I drew back the bedcovers, he handed me the towel, crawled in, and lay on his stomach. I pulled the covers back up to his waist, wiped absently at myself and tossed the towel. I put antibiotic cream on his back, then carefully taped new bandages in place. I crawled in next to him and settled down on my back, my arm stretched out above his head. He turned his face toward mine.

"Welcome home, Dane." I reached out and touched his cheek. He rested his head on my chest, and I combed my fingers through his damp hair. Suddenly, I choked up.

"I was afraid too," I whispered. I wanted to choke back anything else, but more words came out in a wild rush. "I was so afraid you'd d-die, that I wouldn't get the chance to show you how I felt...."

He lifted his head and swiped at my tears. I put my arm around him and pulled him close, and he kissed my cheek and rested his forehead there.

"I am so sorry I couldn't be honest like you."

"Shh. It's all good now. Go to sleep. You need to sleep."

He dropped his head to my chest, and soon his even breathing drowned out the wind and I could fall asleep too.

NOTHING moved much the next day, especially not the blizzard. I checked in with Jesse and Uncle Karl by phone, built up the fire in the stove, put a chicken in a slow cooker, and waited for Dane to wake up. Now waiting was easy. I could tiptoe into the bedroom ten times an hour if I wanted to make sure he was all right, and I did.

About the time the day was ending and the chicken was smelling good, I heard the shower turn on. I went to work preparing the salad.

"You hungry?" I called when I heard him in the living room.

"Yes."

"Great. The chicken will be done in about thirty minutes."

"I'm not hungry for chicken."

"Do you want something else?"

I walked into the room. He had spread the bedroom quilt atop the rug in front of the stove and was lying naked on his side on top of it.

"I want you." He patted the floor next to his hip.

"Okay then." I stripped out of my clothes and lay on my back beside him. He pulled the lube and some condoms out from under a corner of the quilt and smiled wickedly.

"On your stomach and spread your legs."

I rushed to comply.

He knelt between my legs and his hands teased warm circles across my ass cheeks, raising goose bumps. When I sighed, he kissed each cheek, then bit them. I nearly came right then.

"So nice," he sighed. "So nice."

"Yes." I drew the word out as he began to rub my ass again.

"I had dreams like this when I was gone. Did you, Josh?"

"Yes."

His light strokes changed to hard grabs, and he began to knead my butt like bread dough.

"On your knees now." But I barely had to move. He pulled me up, then put on a condom and cracked open the lube.

He smoothed his hands down my back, and then he was hard against me. He prepped me fast and took me in one long, slow glide that had us both moaning. He stopped to let me adjust to him, but I didn't want to wait. I pushed back hard, thrilled when he growled and thrust deep inside me.

He pulled me up against his chest and snapped his hips, pushing with a force that would have tossed me across the room if he hadn't held me close. I crossed my arms over his and gripped him tightly.

"More. Dane. Please, more." I fell into a frenzy of gripping and pushing back into him, panting and gasping, anything to get him to fuck me harder.

He grabbed my cock hard. "Oh no, cowboy. I've got the reins now, and we don't take off until I say."

He began to move again in long, slow glides and rotations of his hips, hitting my gland each time. A wave of pleasure built in me, surging through my nerve endings with each thrust, rolling backward as he eased back, only to push me higher when he thrust forward again.

Each time, I gasped and my cock throbbed and my pulse hammered in my ears. And he kept on moving.

"You know," he whispered in time to his movements, "I dreamed of plunging so deep inside you that I touched your heart."

"You are," I gasped. "You did, a long time ago...."

He stopped at that, and pulled out completely. I jumped around in a panic to look at him. His whole body was tense, with something like pain etched across his face.

"What? Are you hurting? What's wrong?"

"Please, Josh, fuck me," he whispered, his eyes closed against me.

He flinched when I touched his shoulders.

"You don't want that."

He still didn't open his eyes as he answered. "I do. I want to give myself to you, to make up...."

The hitch in his voice was horrible to hear, something between shame and terror.

"I need to feel you forgive me."

I wanted to gather him in my arms and tell him I'd forgiven him the moment I saw he was all right. Because I had. I loved him too much to do otherwise.

But he needed something else from me. He waited, unmoving.

"Okay." I swept my hand from the crown of his head down his jaw and his neck and his chest. "But I'm in control."

"Yes."

"Good." I stroked his arms, alternating firm and light touches. "You don't give the orders." I reached for another condom.

"Forget the condom. Just you."

The only sound in the room was the pop and snap of the fire in the stove.

"Just you and me," I answered.

"Always." He cupped my face in his hands.

I leaned in and kissed him softly. His lips parted and let me in. Our tongues danced slowly in his mouth, then moved to mine. He brushed his hands across my chest, and I caressed his neck, everything soft and tender and loving like we'd never been before.

Dane laid a series of kisses across my jaw and nuzzled my ear.

"Now, Josh, please, before I chicken out."

I smiled, and pulled back and cradled his face.

"You can chicken out."

He shook his head.

"Okay. On all fours, okay? We won't hurt your back then."

He nodded and followed my instructions. I kissed his shoulders and swept my hands down his back and thighs and up again across his ass. He shivered.

"Relax, just relax. And if you want to stop, let me know. We won't stop for good. Just for as long as you need. Like you do with me when we're playing hard. You understand?"

He nodded.

"Tell me you understand."

I wanted to hear his voice. The first time was so often scary and painful. It could be worse than awful. I didn't want that for him.

"I understand." He sounded calm and sure.

"Good. Now, take a few deep breaths, okay. And with each one, I want you to relax a little more."

I massaged his ass again. I closed my eyes and moved my hands slow and gentle, spreading my feelings for him across his skin with each stroke. I wanted him to understand what he meant to me.

I lay another line of kisses across his back, avoiding the stitches, while slowly spreading his cheeks with my hands. I kissed my way to his hole and then I licked it, all around and in and out. His opening fluttered, inviting me in, and his body trembled.

"I'm going to lube up my fingers now. Lots of lube."

I rubbed my fingers together to take away the cold, then gently kissed his ass again.

I spread his cheeks and touched his beautiful hole. "One finger now, just resting there, smearing the lube around. Nothing big. Feel it? Push out as I push in."

I slipped the tip of my finger inside him and felt the resistance.

"Oh, wow, so wonderfully tight. So sexy. I can't believe this virgin hole is mine and only mine. Push out again."

He moaned as I pushed in up to the first knuckle, but he didn't sound panicked. I twirled my finger around a bit, then pushed a bit deeper.

"How does that feel?"

"Okay." He sounded surprised.

I kissed his back again and cupped my left hand around his balls, rolling them gently in my fingers.

"Ahhh," he sighed.

"Good, right?"

"Mmm-hmmm."

I slipped a second finger in slowly, using more lube. Then I wrapped my left hand around his cock. It was hardening again fast.

"Ahh, you're liking this. Push out now. Good."

I slid a third finger in and his whole body stiffened. "Shhh, that's a normal reaction. You're breathing too fast. Take deeper breaths.... Good. Great."

Soon, he pushed back when I slid in, forcing my fingers deep inside him. I eased them in and out a few more times. Then he began to fuck them himself. I twisted my fingers to scrape against his prostate. He jumped and cried out.

"See what you've been missing? Pretty amazing, isn't it?"

"Do me," he panted. "I want to feel you inside me."

I withdrew my hand and rested my head on his ass while I lubed myself up.

"You tell me if you need me to stop at any time."

"I won't."

I smiled. I put my cock to his hole, and he stiffened like I'd expected.

"Push out now." I pushed inside a little at a time, listening for his response. There was a sharp intake of breath, but I realized it was mine. "Oh wow, Dane. I've never done this bare. I've never felt anything like this. It is so… Oh, God, I'm going to come so fast."

"Don't you dare!"

I froze, and then I laughed. "Who's in control here?"

But I knew the answer. I kissed his back and eased myself in. When he gasped, I stopped.

"It's okay. I'm going to stay right here while you get used to the feeling. It'll help both of us. Breathe deep…. You are so tight. So fantastically tight."

I rubbed my hands up and down his cock. "Mmm. I think you're doing okay. Look how hard my little soldier is."

"Little?" He sounded menacing.

"Big. Big soldier." I rushed to correct myself and slid my hand up and down his erection and twisted at the top.

He moaned in pleasure then, and I thrust slowly in and out and deeper. His muscles grabbed me and I moaned. I could feel him getting into it.

"Harder," he demanded.

I smiled. He was taking over for sure.

I withdrew, then pushed back in fast and hard until my balls bounced against him.

"Harder, cowboy. Ride me now."

I did, in and out, not stopping for a second, hitting his gland each time. His hips thrust up to meet each stroke. When his hands grasped the quilt in a frenzy, I pushed harder. I grabbed his cock again and pulled, but he was the one really steering us and I was glad.

My groans were coming nonstop. My balls buzzed and tightened. Sparks shot up and down my spine.

"Gonna come," I gasped. "Come with me, Dane."

He cried out and I felt his cum spurt across my hand. My own exploded deep inside him as I continued to push in and out in a wild, uneven rhythm.

"I feel it," he gasped in wonderment.

I smiled and slowed to a stop. When my breath calmed, I slid out of him slowly and collapsed back on my heels, resting my forehead on his ass. He rolled on his side and grabbed at me. I crawled into his arms, my back to his chest.

When I had settled into him, he put his lips close to my ear. "I'm here forever, Josh. I promise."

EPILOGUE

The following summer

OUR second week for families of gay kids was in full swing. The first sold out so quickly, we scheduled a second by extending our season.

Aunt Kate was teaching interested boys and girls the finer points of baking, and girls went fly-fishing with Uncle Karl. Jesse taught roping and cutting, and Sarah, who was a Brooks now, led a creative writing workshop. Even Dane was teaching, having turned the calving barn into a woodworking studio for the week. The parents, meanwhile, were enjoying daily Kaffee Klatches with the Kounselor. That one was Aunt Kate's idea.

To the surprise of us all, one of the families signed up for the week had been with us the past three years already. We'd never known their son was gay.

Chase, now eighteen, hopped out of the car on Sunday with a big grin on his face.

"Didn't know there were any gays in Montana," he said to me right away.

"You're looking at one," I replied, smiling.

"Two," said Dane as he put his arm across my shoulder.

"No way." Chase's eyes bugged out as he stared at Dane, and I broke up laughing.

"Gay cowboys and soldiers. I can't believe it," Chase said in mock horror. Then he became serious. "So, will you tell me about the Rangers this year, then?"

"Yeah, I promise," Dane said.

That conversation occurred as we sat around the campfire a couple of nights later. A lot of the guests had turned in early because they were going to Yellowstone the next day, but Chase and his parents, plus Jesse and Sarah, Aunt Kate and Uncle Karl, and Dane and I remained. Jesse and Dane did most of the talking. Chase's parents asked some tough questions, but by the end of the conversation, they seemed okay with Chase's decision to enlist.

Nobody wanted to leave, though, and a couple of smaller conversations began simultaneously. Chase's dad put another log on the fire. The flames leaped high, and we could see each other's faces in the orange glow. I was sitting on the ground next to Dane, leaning back against the log he was sitting on. Sarah and Jesse and Chase were on the log next to me.

"So you got married on May 15," Chase was saying to Sarah. "My dad performed his fiftieth gay marriage that day."

I'd forgotten that Mr. Hayes was a minister. He never seemed like one when he was with us. He joked around a lot and went fly-fishing every day all day.

But Chase's comment captured Dane's attention.

"You perform gay weddings, Phil?" he asked Mr. Hayes.

"It's legal in Iowa," he replied. "And I do commitment ceremonies in other states where it's not yet."

"Could you do one of those for Josh and me?"

Good thing I was sitting down. Otherwise, I'd have fallen. I stared at Dane, but he didn't notice. He was totally focused on Phil's answer.

"I'd love to, Dane. I'd be honored."

Aunt Kate, who had been talking teenagers with Chase's mom, was suddenly totally focused on this conversation. In fact, everyone was still.

"A second wedding," my aunt exclaimed, turning to my uncle. "Both our boys married, Karl. But when?" she demanded.

"Can you pull off the mission on Friday night, Kate? Is three days enough time?" Dane had a real twinkle in his eye as he teased her.

"You could have it by the swim pond at sunset like Jesse and I did," Sarah volunteered.

"Between dinner and dessert," Dane agreed. "That way, dinner's out of the way—"

"And dessert is a cake, of course," Aunt Kate interrupted. "Oh, this will be lovely."

"A great idea," Phil said. Then he turned to Dane and me. "I always counsel my couples, so you boys come visit me tomorrow at my favorite fishing spot around lunchtime."

"We'll be there," Dane said.

"You bring lunch," Phil said.

I still hadn't said anything. I didn't say anything until after everyone else headed indoors, their plans on our behalf floating back to Dane and me as we put out the fire.

"We can use some of the decorations from mine and Jesse's wedding. That would be wonderful," Sarah said.

"We'll invite all the guests, of course," Aunt Kate answered.

"I can't wait to tell everyone," Chase said.

When their voices faded, I turned to Dane. "You've never even said you love me."

He lowered his face to mine like he was going to kiss me. But he whispered instead. "It wasn't just this ranch I fell in love with when Jesse read me your letters all those years ago, cowboy. I realized that on that last mission in Afghanistan.

"At first, I thought it was the ranch, but then I knew I was falling for you too, and your goodness and openness. When I met you at last, I couldn't believe you were still that way and accepting me too. Even when I was broken.

"I was so afraid I'd wreck everything, and I did. But you gave me another chance, and I won't fuck this one up. I love you with all I have, and I promise you'll know it every day of our life together. Forever. "

I couldn't think of a thing to say after that.

So Dane and I got hitched Friday night. We weren't really married, not yet. But we pledged to love and cherish each other till death do us part. Jesse stood up with Dane, Sarah with me. My aunt cried and my uncle smiled. And just on time, the sun setting over the Gallatins turned the tops of the Absarokas pink, and the first stars began to shine. My favorite time of the day.

Forever.

Raised in the Midwest, LISA M. OWENS now lives in Josh Brooks's beloved Paradise Valley in southwest Montana. Her husband, two dogs, and The One and Only Cat run the place so she can concentrate on writing. Visit her at http://www.lisamowens.com or on Facebook at https://www.facebook.com/AuthorLisaMOwens.

MORNING
REPORT

SUE BROWN

CPSIA information can be obtained at www.ICGtesting.com
Printed in the USA
BVOW022133090713

325495BV00007B/261/P

9 781623 800444